Arizona Angel

Arizona Angel

Colleen L. Reece

Thorndike Press • Chivers Press
Waterville, Maine USA   Bath, England

This Large Print edition is published by Thorndike Press, USA and by Chivers Press, England.

Published in 2002 in the U.S. by arrangement with Colleen L. Reece.

Published in 2002 in the U.K. by arrangement with the author.

U.S. Hardcover 0-7862-4081-4 (Candlelight Series)
U.K. Hardcover 0-7540-4874-8 (Chivers Large Print)
U.K. Softcover 0-7540-4875-6 (Camden Large Print)

Reece, Colleen

Arizona angel /

Colleen L.

Reece

L.P

1072620

British Library Cataloguing-in-Publication Data available

Library of Congress Cataloging-in-Publication Data

Reece, Colleen L.
    Arizona angel / by Colleen L. Reece.
        p. cm.
    ISBN 0-7862-4081-4 (lg. print : hc : alk. paper)
    1. Women pioneers — Fiction. 2. Arizona — Fiction.
    3. Large type books.   I. Title.
    PS3568.E3646 A88 2002
    813'.54—dc21   2001056373

Arizona Angel

Chapter 1

Angela Cartwright shivered and pulled her heavy cape closer as she lurched against the side of the rocking stagecoach. Though it was midsummer, the early morning Arizona air was cold. She had boarded the stage at Flagstaff for her last miles of the journey from the east coast. The road had become progressively rougher until she felt as if every bone in her body were dislocated.

The only thing making the trip bearable was the thought of Abe waiting in Broken Rail. Her tense lips smiled and warmth flowed into her veins. Abe! How dear he seemed, how glad she would be to reach him!

"What th—" The driver's muttered curse broke in half. Spang! Angela sat upright. Spang! Rifle shots! She threw herself to the floor of the coach, vaguely aware of the driver slumping. The horses, unchecked, raced down the narrow trail, pulling the heavy stage after them. Spang! The horses leaped, and Angela was tossed around the coach like a large doll. For a moment, all the stories she had heard in the east came back to haunt her. Was she the victim of an

Indian raid? No, the Indians were no longer on the warpath.

Angela tried to right herself. She would not crouch there to die. She managed to pull herself up, and then she saw him — a lone rider, dressed in black clothing, his face masked with a red bandana. He raced alongside the coach, and when he saw her staring at him, he deliberately raised the rifle and fired.

Angela threw herself to the floor once more as the bullet ricocheted off the window frame. Terrified, she curled into a small ball. *Someone was trying to kill her!* She closed her eyes tightly. Surely it was all a bad dream. This couldn't be the Arizona that Abe had written about so glowingly. For one furious moment, she wondered — was this just a play-acted scheme Abe arranged to initiate her to the west?

But she remembered the driver's surprise. And, even now, the frightened horses continued to pelt down the narrow and rocky road. This was real. The masked horseman had deliberately tried to kill her. Had Abe made enemies? Enemies who would seek revenge by killing his twin sister? But how could anyone have known which stagecoach she was on? Angela heard a harsh laugh coming from a distance.

"Good-bye and good riddance!" the voice said.

With her heart in her throat, Angela dared to peep out the window. The gunman was little more than a speck in the distance, but her heart nearly stopped beating as she braced herself and looked ahead. The horses were headed straight for a right-angle turn, and a stunted growth of trees appeared to be all that stood between the red-rock edge of the sharply turning road and infinity.

Angela threw herself to the bottom of the coach once more. This was the end. The horses, encumbered by the heavy stage, could never make the turn. With her hands over her face, Angela waited. She felt the coach shudder as the horses swung to the left. With a loud snap, something broke.

She could no longer feel the pull of the horses' strong bodies. They had broken free, but the swaying wagon continued straight on its course. There was a slight pause as it hit the stunted evergreens. Then Angela felt herself falling, turning over and over into blackness.

When Angela opened her eyes, she looked around, but she could see nothing. She panicked, wondering if she were dead or blind. The ground was cold beneath her. Gradually, her eyes adjusted to the darkness, and she saw faint glimmers of light. Stars. She almost laughed aloud in relief. She wasn't dead. There were stars above her, filling the sky as she had never seen them before. They provided enough light for her to see around her.

She moved gingerly. There was a sharp pain in her left arm, but otherwise her body simply ached. Gradually, she struggled to her feet, trying to remember what had happened. Then, in a tumble of memories, it all rushed back. The rider, the shots, and that last sickening lurch as the stagecoach went over the cliff. She must have been thrown clear, then lain unconscious all day.

Angela found the stagecoach a few steps away. She shuddered. It was crumpled like a cardboard toy carelessly tossed aside into ruins. If she hadn't been thrown from it . . . She sternly disciplined her trembling lips. She couldn't think about it now. Her face and lips were dry and cracked. The sun must have beaten down on her for hours.

"What should I do now?" she asked the stars, breaking the frightening silence. "If only I could find water!"

She gently touched her lips and tried to moisten them. Was there a canteen on the coach? It was hard to see even by the starlight, but Angela stumbled to the stagecoach. Hadn't she seen the friendly driver tie a water bag up front? She shuddered.

Would the driver still be on the coach? He must be dead. But how could he keep from being thrown off by all that awful jolting? She forced herself nearer, her eyes adjusting to the night.

Trembling fingers reached for the driver's seat. Angela sighed, not knowing whether to be relieved or afraid. The seat was empty. The driver must have been tossed off earlier. Her fingers steadied and continued to explore. Finally, they found the damp canvas of the canteen.

"Oh, I'm so weak!" It took three tries to unscrew the cap, then Angela let the slightly brackish water gurgle down her throat, off her bruised lips, and onto her hands. It was only when she felt slightly refreshed that she caught herself.

"What am I doing? I need this water! I don't know where I am or how long it will be until I'm found."

She quickly capped the container, her heart sinking at how light it felt. Carefully, she untied the canteen and set it against the wheel of the overturned coach. Then she sank to the ground.

"Well, I can't go anywhere until morning!" As if in answer, a mournful cry came from the desert beyond. She shivered, wrapping her sore arms around her knees.

"I'll just stay here. Surely by morning someone will be looking for the stagecoach." She leaned against the wagon wheel, trying to get comfortable, but her head ached and she felt dizzy. It was a wonder she hadn't been killed.

The eerie cry came again, and Angela bolted upright.

"I have to do something to forget it," she whispered. "Maybe if I go back over everything —"

Angela's eyes closed again. Her head throbbed, but she concentrated on all that had gone before. The lonely cry of the desert animal began to fade.

"Miss Angela, I don't know how to tell you." The maid stopped Angela's rush downstairs.

"Tell me what, Missy?" Angela's blue eyes sparkled as she grabbed Melissa around the waist and whirled her in an exuberant dance. "Don't look so glum. Nothing could be that bad!" Angela's red-gold hair gleamed in the ray of sunlight through the curtains.

"If you've scorched my favorite dress, I'll wear another. Captain Forbes likes me no

12

matter what I wear!" A dimple crept into one cheek, but the maid didn't even notice.

"Oh, Miss Angela —" Tears poured down Missy's face. "It's — it's —" Something in the girl's complete despair frightened Angela. She gripped Missy's arms.

"What is it, Missy?"

"It's your daddy and mama." A fresh wave of tears poured down her cheeks. "They —"

"That's quite enough, Missy." A deep voice spoke from the doorway. "I'll take over from here."

With a frightened look of relief, Missy ran for the door, still sobbing. The family lawyer took Angela by the arm.

"You must be brave, my dear. Your parents have both been killed."

Angela stood in frozen silence.

"I don't believe it," she moaned. "They just went to the shore for the day."

"I know." The man sighed heavily. "It happened there. Your mother saw a child fall in the water and leaped to save him. It was a rocky area, unfit for bathing.

"When your father saw them, he dove in, too. Your mother insisted he leave her and take the child to shore. By the time he returned to your mother, the waves were too much for either of them. The child was saved, but your father and mother went down together. The undercurrent was too strong."

Angela didn't move.

"Come, child," the lawyer said. "Let Missy put you to bed. I'll get Doctor Alden to give you something to help you sleep."

"No." She stared at him. "There will be things to do, to take care of."

"Let me handle them," he offered.

Again she refused. "I have to do something. I can't go to bed."

For two days Angela worked stoically, without self-pity or tears, making arrangements for the funerals. Even on the day of the funerals, Angela didn't cry.

"I can't believe it has all happened," she told Captain Forbes, who accompanied her home. "The accident, finding out the house and jewels and even the furniture must all go to pay debts." She caught a quick look from the captain.

"Not that it matters. I wouldn't want to stay in the house without them. It's just that my whole world seems to have been turned upside down. Even the servants will have to go."

"The situation is really that serious?" asked the captain. Angela caught an odd note in his voice.

"Yes. When it's all over, I'll be penniless." She looked directly at him. "Does it make a difference?"

He colored. "Well, I suppose it does. I had thought when everything was over we could marry. Of course, I had hoped there would be a little something —"

He broke off, then continued under her icy stare. "I don't make so much as a captain, and, I'm sure you understand —"

"I understand completely, Captain Forbes." Angela opened the door and waved him out. "Thank you for your — shall we call it kindness? I won't be seeing you again."

"Angela, Miss Cartwright, is that quite fair? Surely you must —"

The closing door shut him off.

"Well, every bridge is washed out behind me," Angela told her lawyer that night. "My parents are gone, Captain Forbes is gone, the servants are gone."

"But what about you?" The keen eyes were piercing, but soft with friendship.

"I am going to Arizona." She pulled a letter from her dress. "Abe wants me to come. He has a little log cabin. I want to be with him!"

The lawyer was struck by the pallor of her skin against the red-gold of her tightly knotted hair and the black collar of her mourning gown.

"You and Abe always were close. But Arizona? Isn't it still uncivilized?"

"I don't care," Angela said. Her eyes showed the first flash of spirit since the accident. "You know Abe went out to become a cowboy. He worked on a ranch but was hurt when his horse stumbled and fell."

Angela's eyes were proud. "He didn't let it stop him. After his leg healed, he looked around for work. Even though he limped badly, he thought he could find some ranch work. Instead, the people of Broken Rail asked him if he would consider teaching their children! They had had a hard time getting teachers. None of them would stay. So, for the past year, he's been teaching."

"And he's just over eighteen years old, like you!"

"Yes. Maybe that's why he's such a success. He's only a few years older than some of his students." Angela fingered the letter from her twin. Her voice lowered.

"Abe writes that he has discovered something important. He doesn't say what. He just says to come. There's a place for me, and I can live with him. Who knows? Maybe I'll even find a job."

Angela lifted her chin as, for the first time,

a few tears spilled down her cheeks.

"He's all I have left."

Propped against the broken stagecoach, Angela again felt the tears. How glad she was that Abe hadn't known which stagecoach would bring her! He would be worried sick if she hadn't shown up on time. In the morning, she would try to climb the cliff and get back to the road. Eventually, she would make her way to Broken Rail.

Her fingers strayed to the letter carefully hidden in her chemise. Nothing in Abe's letters had prepared her for the people and country she had seen.

She had traveled first in the hot, dusty train, crossing rolling hills dotted with sagebrush and stunted cedar and pine. At Albuquerque, she had stared at the Indians and cowboys, her mind whirling. Her eyes had grown tired from trying to look through the windows at the parched land, the Indian hogans, the pitifully inadequate corn patches.

Then the stagecoach ride had begun. Gradually, the desert had given way to distant mountains. At Flagstaff, Angela had sighed with relief. There were trees, many of them, and a white-capped mountain in the distance.

After the stage left Flagstaff, Angela had found herself moving into still a different land, a land with huge red rocks and deep valleys bordered by tall mountains. Could she ever learn to live in such a country?

Angela twisted restlessly. She must go a step further and relive that horrible scene in the coach after the driver had muttered and slumped over. Abe would want to know exactly what had happened.

She reviewed it in her mind. The driver's broken curse, the spang of bullets, the horse and the masked rider. There was something about that rider. No, not the rider. The horse. That was it! There was something about the horse she had to remember. Abe would want to know. It would help him find whoever shot at her. She closed her eyes tightly, trying to remember, but she only succeeded in making her head ache more.

"Tomorrow," she promised herself. "I'll remember it tomorrow," Now she had to stay awake. What if that creature who had cried earlier came and found her sleeping?

As the hours passed and the stars grew even brighter, the girl's lonely vigil became more difficult. Several times she forced herself to her feet to walk from the stagecoach to the big boulder and back. In the darkness, her foot struck something. She staggered and sank to the ground. She could force her tired body no longer. With an exhausted sigh, she curled up in her cloak and slept.

A few paces away, the canteen she had kicked lay on its side. Precious water dribbled from the loosened cap and seeped into a little pool of moisture. The pool was eagerly gulped by the barren, thirsty land.

Chapter 2

Owlhoot Olson leaned forward, placed his scuffed boots on the massive desk in his ranch-house office, and sighed. "Will, I can't afford to lose many more cattle. After that bad dry spell last year, I barely squeaked through. Now —" He waved his hand expressively.

Will Clark's eyes followed Owlhoot's gesture. Through the window lay the hundreds of acres making up the Double O ranch. Horses bearing the brand of the Double O grazed peacefully. In the distance, mountains rose until they met with the sunny Arizona sky.

"I may even have to sell part of the Double O if we don't find the rustlers that're driving off the stock."

"You can't sell!" Will's blue eyes turned fiery.

"I don't know what else to do." Owlhoot's shoulders drooped.

"Owlhoot, how long have you known me?"

"Long enough to know you're the best foreman this spread's ever had. Why?"

"Long enough to trust me?"

Owlhoot's feet came down with a bang.

"You bet your life!"

A slight smile crossed Will's lean, tanned face.

"What would you say to having me buy into the Double O as kind of a silent partner?"

Owlhoot was speechless.

"Why, I couldn't think of anything better. But your thirty a month can't have built up to much."

Will's face was serious as he unflinchingly looked into the other man's eyes.

"Owlhoot, I didn't tell you anything when I first came out here except I was from North Carolina and wanted a job."

The boss waved his mighty hand.

"Enough for me."

"Yeah, and that's why I stayed. What I didn't tell you was that I'm the only son of a North Carolina plantation owner."

Owlhoot's eyes widened in shock.

"I ran off when the girl I planned to marry eloped with someone else. Ellen broke my heart, or so I thought then. Anyway, I left. Never have been back." A somber shadow crossed Will's face.

"Mama died several years ago, and I got this just last week." He held out a crumpled envelope.

" 'Your pa died last week,' " Owlhoot

21

read slowly. " 'Everything he had goes to you. Please advise.' " The date was several weeks old.

Owlhoot wasn't prepared for the spasm of pain in Will's face. In silence, the boss held out his calloused hand, meeting the steel grip of Will Clark.

"Thanks for telling me, Will. I don't suppose you want the boys in the bunkhouse to know about this."

"Nope. It's enough for them to know you've taken on a silent partner. Don't tell them it's me."

A lightning grin chased the darkness from Will's face.

"Especially Red Taggart. He'd never get over spurring me about not shelling out for drinks and smokes every time we git to town!"

An underlying affection came through his words. "You've got a good spread, good hands, grass, everything you need, Owlhoot. My idea is to run in more cattle."

Will motioned to a range map crudely drawn on the wall. "It's bound to get the rustlers excited. And when it does —" he laughed.

Owlhoot's chair crashed, and he leaped to his feet, his face shining. "Put her there, partner!" His handshake was bone-crushing. "I'll get old Beale in town to get some papers ready and —"

"No papers. No Beale."

"Aw, Will," Owlhoot said, "we've got to have papers."

"Your handshake's good enough for me."

"And yours for me. But if anything happened, folks would need to know the ranch is part yours."

Owlhoot rummaged in his desk and pulled out paper and a pen. Then he dipped the pen in an ink bottle, laboriously wrote out an agreement, and handed it to Will.

"Fine," Will said without much interest.

"We'll both sign it just in case anything happens to either of us," said Owlhoot. "You have anyone your share should go to if it comes to that?"

"Nope. It can go back to you."

"All right, then." Owlhoot gruffly picked up the pen and signed his name. But when Will started to add his signature, an involuntary grin tipped up the corners of his mouth.

"What's so all-fired funny?"

Will made no effort to control his mirth. "I sure wouldn't have guessed your name was Oliver!"

"It ain't," Owlhoot bellowed like a charging bull. "As far as this ranch and Arizona are concerned, I'm Owlhoot." He glared at his friend. "Got that?"

"Got it." Will signed, handed the paper back to Owlhoot, and watched him put it into the safe in the wall behind the desk. Will was still grinning as he retrieved his big hat and sauntered toward the door, spurs jangling.

"So long for now — Oliver!" He laughed out loud and ducked out the door.

"What's so funny, Will?" Red Taggart was leaning on the corral bars watching Vaquero break a horse.

"Nothing much. Just been chewing the fat with the boss." Will looked the rangy rider up and down, seeing the sweat stains on his hands. "Been helping Vaq?"

"Naw. Just got in from checkin' that draw between here and Broken Rail." Red ran a grimy hand through the carrot top that had given him his nickname. "Hey, Will, any chance of borrowing Apple Pie for an hour or so?" He turned a deep, dull red under Will's stare.

"I know you hate loaning that horse, Will, but he's the fastest thing on the range. Owlhoot wants a wagon part as soon as he can get it. With Apple Pie, I can be in Broken Rail and back before any of the other horses can be caught and saddled."

Will's answer was short. "You can take him, but if I catch you bringing him back in sweating the way you usually do a horse, I'll break every bone in your body!"

He turned and stalked away. He hated loaning Apple Pie, Red was right about that. But most of the good horses were on the range being worked with the cattle.

"Thanks, Will!" Red whooped and loped toward the corral. Riding Apple Pie was something to brag about. "Out of my way, Vaq, I'm comin' through!"

Will felt uneasy as he watched Red ride away on Apple Pie. He almost called him back, then he laughed at himself. My, he was getting to be cantankerous!

Of all the hands, Red was the one closest to him. They had shared blankets and grub, ridden night watch together, fought rustlers. When Will had ridden away from Ellen and North Carolina, he had been determined never to get close to anyone again. But gradually Red had become the brother he'd never had.

Will leaned on the top fence rail and watched Vaquero finish working the horse. The dusky man was hot and tired. He slid down, holding the reins of the meekly following bay lightly in one hand.

"Whew! Hot work!" Vaq mopped his face

25

with his bandana. "But I like it!" White teeth gleamed in an infectious grin.

"Good work, Vaq. Take him to the others." Aimlessly, Will wandered back to his log cabin. When he'd been made foreman, he'd been given a separate cabin instead of a place in the bunkhouse. It suited him well.

He liked the hands, worked with them, slept in blankets on the ground along with them when they were on roundup. But when they were working closer in, Will liked a place of his own. Crude shelves held stacks of books, his companions for evenings in front of the fireplace. He ate in the cookshack, but the cabin was his own.

On impulse, Will turned from the porch and looked over the range. He loved it and always had. His dream, once he came to Arizona, was to be a ranch owner. Now it was with new eyes that he scrutinized the lush grass giving way to sage and cedar, the rolling hills that ended in mountains, the red-rock canyons splitting the earth. He breathed in the sage-scented air and watched the sprawling white ranch house, partially screened by cottonwoods, catching the sun's rays.

Arizona! Let others have their cities. He'd take the range. A North Carolina cowboy.

Will grinned at the thought.

Yet, even while he surveyed the ranch with satisfaction, part of Will listened for the rhythmic beat of hooves that would signal the return of Red and Apple Pie. His mouth set in a hard line. No more. Never again would he loan Apple Pie, even to Red. Apple Pie was too good a horse to have to serve more than one master.

"Ho, Will!" Red's yell came from the hard-packed road in front of the corral. He swung to a stop and patted Apple Pie. "What a horse! No wonder you hate to lend him!"

"I don't intend to ever again."

Some of the smile died from Red's eyes. "Don't blame you. I won't ask again, either."

"Did you get the part Owlhoot wanted?"

"Funny thing. It wasn't ready when I got there!" Red shrugged. "Better get to work. Want me in the south field?"

"Yup," Will agreed. But as Red swung away, Will's forehead wrinkled. Something was funny about Red and the trip. Why did Owlhoot send him if the part wasn't ready? Well, he didn't have time to worry over it. Too much work to do. No loafing around when he was half-owner of the sweetest little spread west of the Rockies!

Twenty-nine years old, ranch owner, everything he could want right here in Arizona — what would Ellen think if she could see him now?

By the time the day was over, Will and the other men were drooping. They'd combed draws, chased cattle, and finally ridden back in for supper and sleep. Over dinner, Red complained, "If ever I git to heaven and there's a cow in sight, I'm goin' to turn right around and hightail it for hell."

"Haw haw! You git to heaven?" One of the hands snickered.

"If I wasn't so tired, I'd massacre you." Red glared down the long table. "Hey, Cookie, where's the grub?"

The ranch cook shoved platters on the table, his red face beaming. "Steak. Biscuits. Spuds and gravy. Beans. Fresh tomatoes."

"Aw, what's for dessert?"

"Apple pie and cream." He was drowned out by the approving yells.

"One thing, the Double O's got the best cookie around," Red bragged, through a mouthful of tender steak.

"Yeah," Will said, as he ladled gravy over the potatoes and speared sliced tomatoes. "Sure glad Mrs. Olson has that vegetable garden. These tomatoes are big as moons."

"You goin' to town tonight?" Red asked.

"Town?" Will laid down his heavy steel fork and stared. "After the day we put in?"

"I am." Red's eyes didn't quite meet Will's.

"Maybe the wagon part will be ready," Will said.

"Maybe it will. I'll stop by and see." Red was nonchalant as he shoved back his chair. "Any of you boys with me?"

"Sorry, boys, no one's going to town tonight." Owlhoot stood in the doorway with fire in his eyes.

"Laramie just came in from the north range half shot to death. Rustlers again. Got away with another fifty head of cattle."

Immediately, supper was forgotten. In five minutes, the hands were riding hard toward the north range. Laramie was the first to be hurt. Losing cows was one thing, but having one of their buddies shot was another.

Through the long hours of the night they rode, grim-faced, searching for any trail the rustlers might have made. Just before dawn, Will called a halt.

"Rest. We'll go on after daybreak."

It was in those few minutes out of the saddle that Owlhoot dealt the crushing blow. Looking at the weary cowboys, he said, "There's a two-faced, rotten skunk on the Double O."

"What!" The men sat up straight, staring at their boss.

"It's true." Owlhoot's face and voice were heavy. "Laramie told me. He was half killed when he got in. I don't see how he ever stayed in the saddle. He could only tell me that he'd seen some of the horses before the rustlers shot him. *One of them was wearing a Double O brand.*"

"I don't believe it! None of our outfit would be so low!" Red turned to face the boss, eyes blazing. "I just don't believe it!"

Will let out the breath he'd been holding. For one awful moment, he had remembered Red riding away on Apple Pie. But now the anger in Red's face burned away all suspicion.

If any man on earth was innocent of being in that rustler gang, it was Red. No guilty man could come up with such a furious expression.

"All right!" Red had whirled to face them all, both guns snatched from his holsters and held low. "We'll find out right now who it is. Swede? Vaq? Slim?" The guns leveled at one after another.

"You crazy fool, put up those guns!" Will leaped into the circle of firelight. "What's

30

the matter with you?"

"We're an outfit," Red said stubbornly. "If there's a snake in it, we've got to get rid of it."

"Not this way. We'll wait until Laramie can tell us."

Slowly, Red sheathed his guns, the fire dying from his face. "Sorry, boys," he shot an apologetic glance at them all. "Guess I went out of my head."

His face hardened again and his eyes shone. "But when Laramie tells us who it is —" He touched the gun butts. He didn't have to finish his sentence.

But Laramie never told them who had been riding the Double O horse. By the time the hands returned to the ranch, saddle-sore and worn out, Laramie was dead.

"Somebody's going to pay for this." Red spoke the final words later that day at Laramie's burial. "Laramie was one of us."

Silently nodding, the others stood with bared heads, then one by one drifted back to the bunkhouse. There was no revelry that night, no hollering at Cookie. The men sat silently in the bunkhouse and tried not to look at Laramie's empty bed.

Will stood with Owlhoot watching the sliver of moon rise. "It's hard to believe, isn't it?"

"Laramie sounded so positive, I couldn't doubt him." Owlhoot sighed heavily. "Still want to buy into the Double O, Will?"

Will's shadow was long and steady as he lounged on the porch. "Yep."

Owlhoot's strong hand reached out and the silent clasp showed more than words could have said.

The two men sat and listened to the night sounds of cattle moving in a nearby field, a cricket under the porch, the swish of grass in the night wind. "I have a feeling we're in for a long spell," said Owlhoot.

Suddenly, iron fingers gripped Owlhoot's wrist. Without a word, Will pulled him back into the shadows. There was a slight rustling in the cottonwoods, then silence. Neither man moved. A figure stepped out from behind a tree, hesitated, then slipped behind another tree closer to the porch.

"Wait here," Will whispered. Stopping to pull off his boots, he crept toward the figure, now moving, now still. When he was within yards of the black-clad shadow, Will stopped and waited.

The unknown visitor moved closer to the porch. Step by step, Will followed.

"Stop right there!" His low command froze the figure in place, then, with a wild dash, it ran up the steps toward the front door. Will overtook it, clamping strong hands around the head, over the mouth.

"Open the door, Owlhoot!"

The black-covered figure gasped and struggled, kicking and biting. Owlhoot flung open the door.

Will carried his still-struggling burden inside and deposited it in the center of the lamp-lit room.

"What the —"

"A woman!"

Owlhoot and Will's voices joined in astonishment. The figure righted herself and threw back the dark hood. Red-gold hair tumbled to her shoulders, and eyes as blue as Will's blazed with terror.

Chapter 3

Panting, trembling, she took one step back from the two men.

"Miss —" Will started for her.

"Stay right there!" Her frail hand thrust out at him. "If you come one step closer, I'll scream and bring every person on this ranch, including the owner!"

Owlhoot gulped. "I — I *am* the owner."

"Is it an old Arizona custom to creep up on visitors in this part of the country?" Fury was fast replacing fear in the girl's face.

Will found his voice. "Is it your custom to creep up on a home after dark instead of coming straight to the front door?"

Angela swayed on her feet. "It's just that I'm so tired —" She steadied herself against the wall with white-knuckled fingers. Her courage was fast dissolving.

"You Arizonians do welcome people in the strangest way. First, my stagecoach driver was killed and I was shot at and the coach went over a cliff and —"

"What are you saying?" Will grabbed her shoulders and glared at her. "Are you out of your head?"

Some of the luster disappeared from

Angela's eyes and she sagged in his grip.

"Perhaps I am." Her laugh was hollow. "Come to Arizona, Abe said —"

"Abe?" Will's mind reeled. "Then you're Abe Cartwright's twin sister, the one who's coming."

"Wrong. The one who's here." She swallowed a sob. "If I might sit down, I've had quite a day."

"What on earth's going on in here?" Mrs. Olson stood in the doorway. Sympathy was etched into every motherly line of her face. "Will Clark, what are you doing to that poor child?"

Will could feel his face redden. "Why, I guess I'm just holding her up."

"Well, don't! Get her on the couch over here and I'll get her something to eat." Mrs. Olson's keen eyes took in what the surprised men had failed to see.

"She's all torn up. Must have come a long way."

For the first time, Owlhoot and Will noticed the torn cloak, the scuffed shoes, the dirty face and scratched hands. Angela could feel their stares, but she was past caring. All she wanted to do was close her eyes and sleep.

"Now, Miss Cartwright," Will guided her to the couch. "You just stay there until

Mom Olson gets some grub. Then we'll want to hear all about it."

Angela closed her eyes tightly to prevent the tears from seeping through. By sheer willpower, she forced her body to still and her trembling fingers to relax. Somewhere in the distance, she heard a troubled voice.

"She's all right, isn't she, Will?"

"Sure. Just tuckered out."

The soft warmness of a blanket felt heavenly, and even Angela's mind became still. By the time Mrs. Olson bustled in with hot soup, Angela was almost asleep.

"Wake up, child. You need hot food first, then you can sleep."

"We want to hear her story," Owlhoot said.

Angela opened her eyes in time to catch Mrs. Olson's glare.

"Not tonight you won't! She's going to eat and get to bed. Time enough tomorrow for whatever she has to say."

"That's just one more night a killer's on the loose."

Mrs. Olson indignantly drew her ample frame up tall. "You can't do anything tonight. This girl's got to rest!"

Owlhoot threw up his hands. "No arguin' with you, Mom. Feed her and bed her and we'll talk in the morning. Come on, Will. We'll just see if —"

Angela lost the rest of the sentence through the closing door.

"Eat." Never had she been so willing to obey. The homemade soup tasted wonderful. She emptied the bowl as Mrs. Olson watched.

"More?"

"No, thanks." Angela sank back to the couch.

"Come on, then," Mom Olson said gently, helping Angela up the stairs to a spotlessly clean room. Delving into an old chest, she brought out a soft, warm nightgown.

"Let me wash your face first." The cloth she dipped in the basin nearby was as soft as her touch. "Sleep, child." With a smile, she blew out the kerosene lamp and closed the door part way.

Again tears crowded Angela's eyes. "Thank you."

Mrs. Olson paused in the doorway. "I'm just sorry you had such a bad introduction to Arizona, child. Don't judge us all by what's happened. You'll see Abe tomorrow, and Will and Owlhoot will get to the bottom of all this."

She hesitated.

"Just one question. Did you see the driver afterwards?"

"No, I couldn't find him."

"All right. Goodnight, child." With a rustle of billowy skirts she was gone.

The bed was heaven after the night on the hard ground. Angela snuggled deep under the patchwork quilt, curled into a ball, and slept.

It seemed as if she'd barely closed her eyes when she felt a strong beam of light warming her face. Cautiously, she opened her eyes and peered at the sun shining through the tiny opening between the curtains. What time was it?

Barefoot, she padded to the window. The ranch house was still, but she could hear sounds outside. Throwing back the dainty curtain, she gazed down on the corral. Mr. Olson and Will were leaning against the fence, deep in conversation. Nearby, two saddled horses waited.

Hastily, Angela climbed into her clothing. The cloak had protected her long dress, and, somehow, in the night the dress had miraculously been sponged and pressed. Had Mrs. Olson stayed up all night working? With the aid of the comb and brush laying out on the dresser, Angela gathered her glorious hair into a careless knot at the nape of her neck. The scratches on her face had diminished in color, and, oddly enough, she felt almost like her old self.

"Anyone home?" Angela softly walked down the stairs and peeked into the room where she had been carried the night before.

"In here." She followed the sound of the voice to the big kitchen. Mrs. Olson smiled at her and lifted a pan of wonderful smelling buns from the oven.

"For your breakfast," the woman said.

"Oh, Mrs. Olson, you shouldn't have gone to so much trouble!"

"Sure I should. I like to bake, and it's about time for Owlhoot and Will to come in for a second cup of coffee." She poured the coffee into thick mugs.

"Well, Mom, she looks a bit different this morning, don't she?"

Owlhoot's laughing remark spun Angela around. Behind him stood Will Clark. She hadn't realized last night how tall Will was, or how strong. She'd seen the blue eyes, but hadn't noticed his wavy, brown hair or his big, gentle hands. Catching the admiring look he gave her, she blushed and reached for a roll.

"Better have a hot roll, Mr. Clark, before they're all gone!" she teased.

"Haw haw!" Owlhoot's big laugh filled the kitchen. He stopped abruptly, though, when Angela spoke.

"Have you heard anything about my

driver?" she asked.

Will exchanged glances with Owlhoot.

"Eat your breakfast first, Miss Cartwright," Will said. He deliberately smiled at her. "You see, once *I* get started on those rolls —"

Angela's heart dropped. So there was news. She silently picked at her food until she thought the men were satisfied that she'd had enough.

"Now, Mr. Clark," she said, "please tell me what you've found out."

"My friends call me Will," he said, as he ushered her into the living room. The Olsons followed.

Will's face became sober.

"I rode into town early this morning, Miss Cartwright. I found your stagecoach driver. He's put up over at Doc Bennett's sister's house.

"He was thrown clear before the coach went over that cliff. He's hurt, but he'll live."

"I'm glad!"

"The only thing is — he couldn't remember any details. Said he was driving as usual when all of a sudden he felt something hit him, and the next thing he knew he was in Dr. Bennett's office."

Angela's face paled. "Then he didn't see

40

the masked rider or hear the bullets or anything?"

"I'm afraid not," said Will. "One of the ranchers on his way to town found the driver lying by the road and loaded him up in his wagon."

Will leaned forward, deadly serious.

"Miss Cartwright, I want you to start at the beginning and tell us everything that's happened since you decided to come to Arizona."

"That's a pretty big order! Why would my coming to Arizona have anything to do with what happened here?"

Will's face turned grim. "I don't know, but I intend to find out." He paused, then said again, "All right, Miss Cartwright, let's have your story."

Angela leaned back, her mind whirling. Then she pulled herself together and began.

"It all started when my parents died in a drowning accident. They were wonderful people, but they never saved a penny. Papa had a good job, as well as an inheritance from my grandfather, so we never lacked for anything.

"Mama and Papa spent their money freely — we lived a rich life. But when my parents died, they left all kinds of bills. We had to sell everything they owned to pay off their debts."

Hastily, Angela described the confusion she felt after losing her parents and her home. She briefly explained her final decision to go to Arizona to live with Abe.

She omitted mention of Captain Forbes and his greed. And she didn't dwell on her long train trip. But when she mentioned Albuquerque, her face lit up.

"My journey really started there. The closer I got to Broken Rail, the more exciting it was.

"But then, after we left Flagstaff that morning, the nightmare started. I heard a shot and saw the driver slump over in his seat. The horses started running out of control. There were other shots."

Angela's face was colorless, reflecting the horror she'd felt.

"I stayed down most of the time. But once I peeked out the window. I saw a rider with a bandana over his face. He raised his rifle and pointed it directly at me!"

Will swallowed hard, but Angela didn't notice. "I threw myself back to the floor and stayed there. I knew the horses were running away, but I was helpless to stop them.

"Finally, I heard someone laugh and call out 'good-bye and good riddance!' I looked out the window again, and this time I saw the curve. I knew the horses couldn't make it."

She bit her lip.

"I remember thinking I didn't want the horses to die. Just then, I heard something snap. The horses turned — but the stage didn't. I remember trying to hang on to the seat, and then — nothing. I don't remember anything else until I woke up. When I opened my eyes, all I could see was darkness.

"At first, I thought I was dead or blind. I finally realized it was night. My head ached so —" Her fingers crept to her head.

In an instant, Mrs. Olson was beside her, examining the lump. "Land sakes, child, why didn't you tell me you had this knot?"

Angela managed a wan smile. "I guess I forgot it after everything else."

"Were you still inside the stagecoach when you woke up?" asked Owlhoot.

"No, Mr. Olson, I was thrown clear," she shuddered. "It's a good thing because the stagecoach was completely shattered. I slept until dawn, then looked for the water bag. I must have knocked it over in the night. All the water was gone." The three listeners again exchanged glances. This young woman was luckier than she knew.

One dimple flashed. "I knew better than

to stay in the Arizona sun too long." She frowned.

"I was already parched, and my skin and lips were cracked and dry. I knew I had to get back up to the road, but that cliff looked awfully high.

"I didn't know if I could make it, but I knew I had to try. I thought about how terrible Abe would feel if he found out I'd died in the desert after he sent for me. I crawled up the side of the cliff, using every bit of brush and rock for balance. I didn't look back. I hate high places."

Will Clark brushed his eyes as he imagined the valiant figure of the girl, encumbered with her long dress and black cloak, trying to crawl up that cliff.

"I was so tired when I got to the top. I didn't know what to do. It was so hot. I crawled under a tree and must have fallen asleep. The sun was starting to go down when I woke up again. I began to walk down the road. I thought surely someone would be coming that way! But no one came.

"I was almost to a fork in the road when I heard horses coming. I panicked! What if one of them was the man who had tried to kill me? I crept into a bush and waited. Every story of rattlesnakes and scorpions came back, but I was more scared of who the men might be."

Angela saw the rigidity of Will's set jaw and hastened to add, "The men didn't see me. They rode to the fork and turned to the south, down the road marked *Broken Rail*. It was still light enough for me to see an old painted sign standing by the road to the north. The sign read *Double O Ranch*.

"I thought surely there would be people at the ranch who would help me! So I ran up the road to the left. I finally saw the light in the window, but just then I heard more horses. What if those men were after me? If only I could reach the house without being seen! I crept from tree to tree, and — you know the rest."

"I grabbed you." Will's head was bent in apology.

"I don't blame you."

The softness of Angela's voice drew Will's eyes to hers like a magnet.

"Anyway, I'm here," she said.

"Miss Cartwright?" asked Owlhoot, looming over her. "Is there anything, anything at all, that could help you identify the man who shot at you?"

Angela was silent for a long moment, pressing her fingers to her temples, trying to remember.

"Yes, there was something, Mr. Olson.

45

But I don't remember what! I don't remember anything. I could see the rider again and never even know that he was the one who tried to murder me!"

"For heavens sake, Owlhoot, are you trying to scare her to death?" chided Mrs. Olson.

Owlhoot slowly looked into his wife's indignant face.

"No. I'm trying to protect her in case someone tries to hurt her again. Angela, whoever tried once to kill you may try again — if he thinks you recognized him in any way. Lynching's too good for a skunk like this one, and he'll know it."

Owlhoot took one of her hands in his own rough one. "I just want you to be careful."

"She won't have to be. I intend to find out who did this," Will said quietly. Angela was struck by the determination in his voice.

"Something's pretty fishy if you ask me," Will continued. "No one knows Miss Cartwright, yet someone tries to kill her. It must be because of something they think she knows."

"But what could I know — oh!"

"What is it?" Will eyed her. "Anything you can remember may help us. Your life may depend on it, Angela."

Angela's voice faltered. "It's just that Abe

46

wrote and told me he was onto something big. He didn't say what." Her hand flew to her chemise and pulled out a crumpled page. She handed it to Will. He glanced at the letter, then at Owlhoot.

"Nothing here. But that doesn't change things." He abruptly pulled on his riding gloves.

"Miss Cartwright, how soon can you be ready to go into town? I'll get the buckboard out. I want you to have a little talk with the sheriff right away, and I want to see that brother of yours. Maybe he can give us a clue as to why anyone would attack you. Did you say the gun man called out, 'good-bye and good riddance?' "

"Yes," Angela whispered.

"Then someone counted on your dying in the wreck. Someone's going to be mighty surprised when we drive into Broken Rail," Will scowled, his handsome face settling in hard lines. "I can't see why Abe hasn't been out here!"

"Hold it, Will," Owlhoot clapped him on the shoulder. "No one except the killer and the driver knew Miss Cartwright was in that stage."

"That's right." Will relaxed. "Well, Miss Cartwright, are you ready to go to town?"

Before Angela could reply, the thud of

47

hooves raced across the yard, almost to the porch. The door burst open and a wild-eyed cowboy strode in.

"There's the devil to pay, Will! Abe Cartwright's been shot, and Doc Bennett says if he lives through the day it will be a miracle!"

"Slim!" Will raised his hand in warning, but it was too late.

"Someone got him last night, I guess. That log cabin he lives in looks like a team of wild horses ran through it. Even the mattress was split open. Somebody sure was looking for something!"

A queer, choked cry caught Slim's attention. Angela had risen from the couch and was leaning against the table for support. Her face was chalk-white.

"Sorry to come bustin' in here like this when there's company," Slim doffed his big sombrero. "But the sheriff's calling for every man on the range to git in town to hunt the killer down. If Cartwright dies, there's going to be a hanging."

Chapter 4

"Slim!" Will's roar nearly drowned out the cowboy's words. "This is Miss Cartwright, Abe's sister."

"My —" He swallowed the rest of his sentence, his face turning dull red. "Miss — Miss Cartwright, I'm terrible sorry — that is, Abe's probably all right. Doc Bennett makes everything sound bigger than it really is, and —"

His apology went unnoticed. Angela had run to Will, clutching his arm.

"Take me to Abe!" Her terror-filled blue eyes looked up at him, imploring. "Hurry, please!"

"Slim," Will ordered, "get that buckboard hitched up." He turned back to Angela. "Get your cloak, something for your head. I'll be outside with the buckboard in five minutes!"

"Here, child." Mrs. Olson sprang into action, her face wrinkling in sympathy. "Owlhoot and I will go with you."

Angela paused in the flight upstairs to get her cloak. "No, they need Owlhoot for the posse." Her face crumpled, but she determinedly forced back her tears. "I'd be glad

49

if you would come, though."

Already the woman's busy hands were untying her apron. By the time Angela returned, Mrs. Olson had snatched a shawl and sunbonnet from her room.

"Come on, child. Will's waiting."

Angela stared blindly ahead during the ride into town. Her heart was racing with fear for her brother. The dark pines and red cliffs that normally would have made her exclaim in wonder flew by unnoticed. She was only aware of Mrs. Olson hanging on for dear life and Will Clark's set face stonily turned ahead as he urged every bit of speed from the horses.

Angela spoke only once, when they slowed at the fork in the road. "That's where —" Her voice failed her.

Mrs. Olson silently patted her shoulder. For a moment, Angela wanted to bury her face in the ample lap and cry out every tear she'd held back since her parents' deaths. But she knew she must not. If she once lost control, she could never face Abe.

Finally, they reached the edge of Broken Rail. The horses raced into town, kicking up enough dust to cloud the old log buildings.

With a mighty "whoa," Will pulled the horses to a stop in front of Doc Bennett's office. Will leaped down from the buckboard and swung Angela down after him. Then he paused to help Mrs. Olson.

Angela ran ahead and rushed through the heavy timber door. A dark-eyed man greeted her.

"Miss Cartwright?" he said. "I'm Doc Bennett. Come with me."

Clutching her cloak, Angela followed the doctor through a pair of heavy curtains that veiled a doorway. Her eyes widened as she entered the back room. This couldn't be Abe, her beloved twin. Not this gray-faced man with the bloody bandage crossing his chest.

"Abe!" Angela ran to his cot. Was he already dead? He looked so still, so helpless. A rush of all the love they'd shared filled her heart.

"Abe, it's Angela!" Her voice did what Doc Bennett had been unable to do. It roused the wounded man from his stupor.

"An— Angela?" The waxen lids opened, revealing a stir of interest in the blue eyes that were so like her own. "You here? Yeah, sent for Angela. Something to tell her."

"Don't try to talk," she begged. "We'll talk when you're better."

A slight smile crossed his face, then twisted in a grimace of pain. "No time. Got to tell you. Now. He got me —"

"Who got you, Abe?" Angela clutched his arm in her intensity. "Who did it?"

"Don't know. Waiting when I got home. Tore up house. Didn't get it, didn't get it, Angela!"

"Didn't get what?"

She cast a despairing glance at Doc Bennett, who was holding Abe's limp hand. The doctor shook his head and gravely whispered, "Let him talk."

"Abe, what didn't he get?"

The flickering light in his eyes steadied.

"Alone — want you alone." Instantly Doc turned toward the doorway. "I'll be just outside if you need me."

"Is he gone?" Each word was labored now. Abe was having trouble speaking, but with a mighty effort, he roused himself and gripped Angela's hand.

"He's gone, Abe. Tell me what the man didn't get."

"Something big." His voice died to a whisper. "Gold. It's —"

"Where, Abe?" Frantically, Angela leaned closer, her ear next to his mouth. If he could tell her, perhaps he would rest. He must get it off his mind.

"It's — I hid it —" he was rambling now. "Tired, so tired. Tell you when —" his head dropped back.

For just one moment, Angela laid her head on his chest. Then she raised her head to search his face. Abe's eyes had closed.

"Doctor Bennett!" Her call brought him through the curtains, closely followed by Will and Mrs. Olson.

Doc bent low, listened, picked up Abe's wrist again, then shook his head. Gently, he freed Angela from the fingers still clutching her hand and beckoned to Mrs. Olson.

"Come, child."

Angela's eyes were dark with horror. "You don't mean —"

"There's nothing you can do for him now." Mrs. Olson led her to the vacant waiting room, pulling the unresisting girl into her arms.

"There, now, go ahead and cry."

The dam broke as Angela sobbed against Mrs. Olson's shoulder. Her handkerchief grew sodden, and Mrs. Olson replaced it with her own. It wasn't until Doc Bennett and Will came back in the room that Angela was able to stop crying.

Will came close, his brown hair tousled from their ride into town.

"Miss Cartwright, I know this has been terrible for you, but if there's anything you can tell us that might help —"

Angela swallowed convulsively.

"Abe said he had something big. He had it hidden, but he didn't say where."

Some strange lock on her tongue kept her from blurting out the word *gold*.

"That's it!" Will stepped back. "He must have found something out that someone didn't want known. Probably wrote it out and hid it somewhere. Somebody knew he had it and tore up the cabin to get it. Abe came in while the thief was there."

"So the thief killed him," said Angela, bitterly.

"So he did." Will looked directly at her, his eyes turning to steel.

"Mrs. Olson, you take care of her. I'm going over to Abe's cabin and nose around, see what I can find."

"All right," agreed Mrs. Olson, "then I'll take this child to the hotel. It ain't much, but it does have clean rooms. You can pick us up there when you're ready. But don't make it too long, Will."

Angela watched Will's straight back and easy walk as he went out the door. Then she let Mrs. Olson lead her away.

Abe was dead. Nothing else mattered. Life seemed too terrible to bear. Angela stumbled into the small hotel room and collapsed on the clean white bed. She made no protest as Mrs. Olson removed her dusty shoes and covered her with a light blanket. In a matter of minutes, the exhausted girl was asleep.

Will Clark reached the little log cabin next to the schoolhouse and kicked open the door. He gasped at the sight. Will had seen some torn up places — bunkhouses after a fight, barrooms when some wild cowpuncher had started a brawl, but this beat all.

Nothing in the room was intact. The mattress was slit and sliding to the floor. Pictures were smashed. Even the water bucket was upside down with the dipper thrown out of it.

"Whew!"

"That's what I say!"

Will whirled to meet the steady gaze of Owlhoot Olson. "Did you ever see such a mess?"

"Not me," said Owlhoot. "I hear young Cartwright's dead."

"Yeah." Will turned away to keep Owlhoot from seeing his face. "Pretty hard on the girl. Wonder what she'll do now."

"She'll come to us for as long as she cares to stay," Owlhoot said firmly. He stepped across the room and picked up one of the smashed pictures. "Good, isn't it?"

Will looked at the scratched and dirty photograph. It was Angela, with a joyful smile Will had never seen. "She's prettier than the picture."

"Sure is. Why don't you just rope and brand her, Will? That is, after all this mess is cleared up," Owlhoot hastily added.

"Right now, Owlhoot, let's get the sheriff and have him take a look at this. Abe told the girl he was onto 'something big.' We don't know whether the thief found it or not. If not," Will steadily met Owlhoot's eyes, "it could mean he'll try again. And there's no one left to try except Miss Cartwright."

"They won't get her, Will."

"They must be pretty desperate."

Owlhoot's eyes shone. "Then she's to be guarded day and night until we find out who did this." The grip of the two men's hands confirmed his words.

The clink of a spur snapped them to attention. "Well, I see you boys beat me to my job." The soft-spoken sheriff stood in the doorway. "Find anything?"

"Nothing. We don't even know what we're looking for." Will repeated what Angela had told them. "It's mighty important to someone."

"Yeah." The sheriff stared at Will. "Is the

girl in any shape to talk?"

"She'll have to be." Grimly, Will told the sheriff what had happened the day Angela came to Broken Rail.

"Someone's going to be mighty surprised — if they haven't already been — seeing her alive and finding out she talked to Abe before he died."

"It appears to me," said the sheriff, "that we'd better just catch this busy gent before he does any more harm." He turned toward the door. "You two with me?"

Owlhoot spoke first. "Will can go. I'll drive the buckboard back with Mom and the girl. You can take my horse, Will." He grinned wryly.

"Yeah, I know she ain't Apple Pie, but old Baldy Feathers will get you there all right. I'll join you later. Right now, I gotta go get the girl."

"I still need to talk to her," said the sheriff.

"Sure, Sheriff. But give her a day or two. Will told you the whole story. I was right there and I heard it."

"She didn't say anything about maybe knowing the masked rider again if she saw him?"

"She thought there was somethin' she should remember, but she couldn't get it back," Will said.

"Tell her if she does remember anything, not to go spreadin' it around," warned the sheriff. "She could be askin' for trouble. This killer could be anyone."

"Aw, Sheriff," protested Owlhoot. "How could it be just anyone? It must be somebody who —"

"Somebody who knew Abe Cartwright well enough to know he'd gotten onto something and that his sister might know about it," declared the sheriff. "Somebody who'd kill for it, maybe twice."

"You think it's the same man who attacked the stage?" asked Will.

"Yeah. And no drifter would know everything this guy seems to know." Spurs clinked again as the sheriff strode out the door.

"Then it's one of us. One of us ranchers or hands who've eaten and slept together," Owlhoot said. "Hard to believe, ain't it?" He suddenly looked old and tired. "I'd rather be dead than come to this."

"Maybe the sheriff's wrong," said Will. But neither Will nor Owlhoot believed it.

"Mom, is she fit to travel?" Owlhoot asked his wife outside Angela's door.

"As fit as she'll ever be. Doc Bennett gave her some pills so she'd sleep. I think she'll be better off with us, don't you? She'll have someone to look after her, just in case." Mrs. Olson's lips tightened. She knew the girl was in danger.

"The buckboard's ready when she is," Will said.

Angela's door slowly opened, cutting off their conversation.

"I'm ready now," Angela said. The sleep had restored a little color to her chalky face, but her eyes were tormented.

"Shouldn't I stay with — with Abe?"

"No! You can't do anything for him now. You've got to get some rest or you'll go to pieces, child. The Double O's far enough away from town so curious folk won't be pesterin' you with questions." Mrs. Olson straightened the girl's collar.

"Fine thing — you coming all the way from back east and having all this happen!"

"Before I go, I have to see the undertaker." Angela blushed. "I don't have much money, but I think there's enough for him."

"You don't have to worry about that." Owlhoot assured her. "Abe was our teacher. It will be up to us, of course, to handle all expenses."

"That's wonderful." A wan smile crossed Angela's face. "I'm very grateful. I really don't have much money. I'll have to get a job as soon as I can."

"A job!" said Mrs. Olson. "Not for awhile. You're going home with us for a nice long visit. Besides, I'd like you to take the job of keeping me company."

"That isn't a job, that's a privilege. But I must find a job when I can," Angela replied. Some of her natural dignity was returning.

"Let's just go home for now, Angela," Mrs. Olson said, gently. "To tell the truth, I'll feel more comfortable getting away from this place and back to the ranch. Never did like towns much."

A faint smile trembled on Angela's lips. What if Mrs. Olson could see some of the towns on the East Coast! She sobered immediately.

"Is there a minister? I'd like Abe to have a Christian burial."

"There sure is," Will said, heartily. "Dandy little preacher comes to town every Sunday. I'll get the sheriff to send a rider over to Outlaw Junction and ask him to come back for the funeral."

Angela's eyes thanked him. "Then I guess there's nothing else for me to do."

Her forlorn voice touched them all.

"Just come on home, honey, where you'll be safe."

Startled, Angela looked at Mrs. Olson. "Safe? Then you think — you think whoever tried to kill me also killed Abe. You think he'll try again."

She knew she should let them know about the gold, but before she could speak, Owlhoot broke in.

"You've got some pretty good protectors."

"I'm handy with a rollin' pin if I do say so myself," Mom Olson bragged, wielding an imaginary weapon. Angela almost smiled again.

"Miss Cartwright," Will stepped closer. "You should face the fact that there's a desperate man around. The sheriff says it must be someone we all know, someone maybe we all trust. It couldn't be a drifter or he wouldn't know about Abe's secret.

"The sheriff also said that if you suddenly remember *anything at all* about who that masked rider might be, don't let on to anyone. Tell me, or Owlhoot, and we'll pass it on to the sheriff. I'm not trying to frighten you, but you must be careful until we catch the killer."

"And if you don't catch him?"

"We will." Will's eyes were steady. "Whoever it is, we'll catch him."

Angela shuddered, but bravely met his intense gaze. "I'll be careful," she promised.

"Drive easy, Owlhoot." Will turned on his heel and was gone.

"Ready, Miss Cartwright?" asked Owlhoot.

"Yes. Oh, wait." A sudden thought struck her. "Would it be possible for someone to find my clothing? The trunk seemed intact yesterday morning, but it was too heavy for me to carry."

"We'll send a rider out when we get home," Owlhoot promised. "Let's go."

There was no hurry going home. Owlhoot let the horses take it easy. He talked about how he and his wife had come and settled in Arizona. He described how the ranch had grown over the years. His voice was soothing. It steadied Angela's nerves.

"You get some rest, child, and I'll bring you up a bite," Mrs. Olson said as they walked into the ranch house. "Put on that gown I gave you and crawl right into bed."

By the time Angela had sponge-bathed and crept into bed, Mrs. Olson arrived with a tray for her. How she'd managed a meal in such a short time was a mystery to Angela. There was chicken breast, ripe sliced tomatoes, a thick-cut piece of homemade bread, even a piece of warm apple pie!

"I talked Cookie out of the pie," Mrs. Olson confessed. She wrinkled up her nose.

"He likes to think he can beat me making pie, but I know better!"

After her meal, Angela closed her eyes and forced herself to remember everything that had happened since she had come to Arizona. Tears flooded her blue eyes as the haunting memory of Abe's face returned to her. She was alone, totally alone. Oh, there were friends back east, but none loved her the way her parents and Abe had. If only she had cousins or aunts and uncles the way most people did! But Angela had no one.

Well then, she decided, it was up to her to make her own way. She couldn't impose on the good-hearted Olsons. There must be some kind of job in Broken Rail!

She shrank from the idea of going elsewhere. At least, here, people had known and respected her brother. If it were true that someone was trying to kill her, then she would be better off here than by herself.

Her worries unresolved, Angela drifted into an uneasy sleep. But soon she was awakened by voices from below. Had Will returned? Had they caught the murderer?

She ran to the window and peered down into the yard. Slim, the cowboy who had burst in that morning, was unloading her trunk. Good! She would have something to wear besides her heavy traveling dress.

She reached to pull the nightgown off so she could dress and go downstairs for her things. But Slim's voice floated through her open window, freezing her in place.

"Owlhoot, I don't know what's goin' on, but it doesn't look good. I'd have been back an hour ago, but I had to put all her stuff back in the trunk. Somebody was there ahead of me! Everythin' she owns was thrown around on the ground. Some of it's torn, like pockets on her dresses. Thought she said her trunk had come through all right."

"She did," Owlhoot answered. "So whoever pawed through Abe's cabin and killed him hasn't found it yet."

"Found what?"

From her place behind the curtain, Angela could hear the sharp suspicion in Slim's question and the anger in the reply.

"I don't know, but we'd better figure it out before there's more killin' here at Broken Rail."

Chapter 5

For one terrible moment, Angela thought she was going to be physically ill. Her groping hand struck the china basin and sent it crashing to the floor. She was still staring at the fragments when Mom Olson rushed in.

"I — I —" The next instant Angela was sobbing in the woman's lap. Gnarled hands, toughened from years of work on the range, stroked the loosened strands of Angela's hair.

"There, go ahead and cry it out, child."

It was the touch Angela needed to release all her emotion. The tears she should have cried earlier drenched Mom Olson's apron. She cried until there were no more tears, then lifted her head and looked straight into the network of kindly creases in Mom's face.

"They —" She gulped back a final sob. "That cowboy, Slim, said my trunk had been opened and my things were all thrown around, and Owlhoot said whoever it was must not have found what he wanted and maybe there'd be more killing."

She blew her nose with the large handkerchief Mom offered.

"Maybe I'd better go back home — only

there's no home to go to."

"Child, you *are* at home, for as long as you want to stay." Mrs. Olson lifted Angela's head.

"You think anyone can hurt you with us here, and with Will Clark around?"

Angela shivered with apprehension. "I don't know. Why would anyone want to kill me?" She thought of what Abe had told her. "Maybe it's because —" Again she wasn't able to share Abe's secret. Owlhoot had appeared in the doorway.

"Did you have to wake her up with your talk?" Mom scolded. "She needs rest."

Owlhoot's keen eyes took in the tear stained face, the fear still haunting the blue eyes. "Sorry. But we'll take care of you, Miss Cartwright."

Something about his quiet assurance and steady gaze settled her more than all the promises Mom had made.

"Bring it in here, Slim," Owlhoot called, stepping out of the doorway.

Slim hoisted Angela's trunk into a corner, then backed awkwardly toward the door. "Miss Cartwright, I'm awful sorry about your trunk and all."

"Thank you," Angela said with a feeble smile. The cowboy escaped before she could say more.

"We're going to find who's doin' all this," Owlhoot said. "And when we do —" He clenched his fists and strode out, his spurs jingling as he walked.

Angela shuddered again. "What a fierce country! How can people stand to live here?"

Mom Olson rose and walked to the window, her profile clear-cut against the view of distant hills and blue sky.

"Don't judge us by what's happened so far, Angela. Arizona is a wonderful place to live. Just because we have skunks and coyotes, some of them the two-legged kind, don't mean the country is bad.

"I reckon there's some of that kind everywhere, even in cities. Maybe more of them in the cities. We don't even lock doors around here. Most of the folks would as soon rob themselves as take anything belonging to a neighbor."

She turned to smile at Angela. "Right now you're hurt and scared, and you should be. But wait until you've met the folks around here and gotten better acquainted. I wouldn't live anywhere else."

She gestured toward the window. "From this window, you can see all the seasons. Fall and its yellow leaves, then winter, and green spring and summer again. You'll find the peace of Arizona in the changing seasons."

Angela couldn't reply. Something was choking her — the sight of this ranch woman who had learned to live in and love what had become a harsh land in Angela's eyes. "I hope I will learn to feel that way," she sighed.

"You will." Mrs. Olson moved toward the door. "Think you can rest now?"

"I'll try."

Angela slipped into bed nestling between the cool sheets as her hostess softly closed the door. Outdoor sounds gradually dimmed until Angela was no longer aware of them.

When she awoke, only a small lamp on the dresser lighted the room. Her tiny watch had stopped. She tiptoed to her door and cautiously opened it, then stepped into the hall. From somewhere downstairs came muted sounds of voices, the clink of cutlery against a plate, a clock striking.

She counted the chimes as she fumbled her way back into the dress she had worn on arrival. Seven o'clock! She had slept all afternoon and evening. She was ravenous!

"Well, howdy!" Will Clark was at the bottom of the stairs as she descended. "You look like you got some shuteye."

A faint color stained Angela's still-white face. "I did. I guess I needed it."

"How about some grub?"

"Grub?"

"Shore." His teeth flashed in a smile. "Food. Supper."

"Oh!" This time the color rose high, and she smiled. "I guess I have a lot to learn about Arizona — even the language."

"You'll do." He looked her over approvingly. "For a gal that's had everything to face that you have in the last few days, you've come through just fine."

His words brought a shadow back to her eyes. "Well, if I'm going to be an Arizonian, I have to learn to live with it." Her smile faded.

"Mr. Clark, Will, did you find —" her voice failed her.

"I found the preacher at Outlaw Junction." His steady gaze held hers, but she saw a muscle twitch in his cheek. "I didn't find the other gent I was looking for — not yet."

Before she could answer, he took both of her hands in his. "Miss Cartwright, we can have the funeral tomorrow afternoon."

It took all her strength to meet his gaze. "That will be fine."

She bit her lips to keep from letting him see how they trembled.

"I don't think I'm very hungry," she said. Her appetite had disappeared.

"You must eat somethin' to please Mom." He gently led her to the kitchen. Mrs. Olson was drying the last of the supper dishes.

"See that she eats a bite, will you? I have to check the horses." He was gone, sliding through the door with his easy swinging walk before she could protest.

"I kept your supper warm, honey," Mrs. Olson said, putting a plate before her. In spite of Angela's protests, the aroma of the homemade beef stew tempted her.

"I'll try."

At first it was almost impossible to swallow. The memory of Abe kept rising to choke her. But she forced herself to eat until her plate was almost clean.

"Good girl." Mom took her dishes to the basin on the cabinet.

"Can't I do my own dishes?"

"Not tonight. When you get settled in, you can help if you like." Busy hands accompanied Mom's smile, and, in short order, the rest of the dishes were done and put away.

"Would you like to sit on the porch awhile? It'll be cool out there." Without waiting for an answer, Mrs. Olson led the way.

"This is nice." Angela leaned her head against a pillar. A lopsided moon offered enough light for her to see Mrs. Olson's face. Finally, Angela spoke.

"We have to talk, you know."

"Why?"

The simple question opened Angela's eyes wide. "I can't just stay here and impose on you."

"Impose? Nobody imposes around here, child. There'll be work aplenty when you're ready for it."

"But I need to earn my keep. I have to work."

Mrs. Olson smiled faintly.

"What can you do? We don't have need of many women out here. Most of us do our own sewing. Widow Bartlett makes the fancy things. We do our own baking and nursing and housekeeping, too. 'Bout the only opening I know of in Broken Rail would be the saloon, and you don't appear to me to be that kind of girl."

"Saloon! You mean dance hall?"

Mrs. Olson smiled again at the naive question. "That's right. I can't see you in the Broken Dollar singing for a living." She glared at Angela. "And worse."

"I can't see me there either." Angela's mouth tipped up at the corner.

"Can't see you where doing what?"

Angela spun around. Will Clark had sneaked up to the porch with catlike grace.

"She's about to run off and get a job, and I was telling her the only job I know of is at the Broken Dollar."

"Broken Dollar! Her?" Something in the lean cowboy's voice warmed Angela.

"Well, she ain't satisfied to stay here with me, and she says she has to have a job." Angela could hear the dry amusement in Mrs. Olson's words.

"It isn't that I don't want to stay here, it's just that I have to make my own way. But I can't really do anything!"

Angela felt the hot blood in her face and was glad it wouldn't be seen in the dim moonlight.

"I never realized before how worthless I am. I can't cook, at least not much. I can't sew or even keep house. But I can learn." Her sturdy assurance collapsed like a pinpricked balloon. "At least I think I can."

She leaned toward Mrs. Olson. "Will you teach me? I'll be here at least until I can find another job."

"Be glad to."

"If you really want a job, why don't you take over your brother's school when it opens in the fall?" Will suggested.

Angela was speechless. Teach school? Abe's school — all six grades in a one-room building?

"Why, that's a fine idea," Mrs. Olson beamed at Will. "If we can't keep her here, that's just it. There's even a log cabin she can have — Abe's cabin."

She broke off, suddenly remembering that Abe was killed in that cabin.

"Sure you wouldn't be afraid to stay there after what's happened?"

"You'd be perfectly safe, Miss Cartwright," Will said. "It's just a few steps from neighbors, right next to the school. You wouldn't even have to get your feet wet in winter. There's a covered porch between the school and the cabin."

Angela forced words through her tight throat. "No, I wouldn't be afraid of the cabin," she said, swallowing hard. "Just of the students."

"Why, you've no need to worry about them. They all loved Abe. They'd be proud to be taught by his sister."

Angela was silenced. She had asked for work. In Mrs. Olson's and Will's minds, it was settled. Angela raised one final protest.

"Maybe I couldn't get the job."

"You'll get it." Mrs. Olson's voice was serious again. "Owlhoot and Doc Bennett and

Mr. Denham — he's the hotel man — they have the say over who is teacher. There won't be any question about it."

"What do you say, Miss Cartwright? Do you want to be Broken Rail's schoolmarm?" Angela could feel Will's searching look. She was saved by Mrs. Olson.

"Will, here we've got her all signed up without even letting her think about it." She rose.

"I've got bread starter to get set. You can talk about it if you like." She went into the house, swinging the door shut behind her. Will sat down on the porch step beside Angela.

"Didn't mean to shove you into something you didn't want." He sounded regretful, yet faintly curious. "If you want to work, though, it's about all there is. Of course, you could always marry me. Then you wouldn't have to work."

Of all the shocks Angela had had since she arrived in Arizona, this was the greatest.

"Marry you?" She felt as if her eyes were standing out of her head on stalks. "Marry you? You don't even know me!"

"I know once you settle in Broken Rail every hand and rancher within fifty miles will be hangin' around trying to catch you. Just thought I'd get my bid in first."

"Of all the amazing —" She choked. "Mr. Clark, I thought you were my friend! Now you've ruined everything!"

He stood, towering over her, and looked at her with his clear eyes.

"Miss Cartwright, this is Arizona. It isn't Boston or New York or any of those fancy places. Out here we work hard. We don't have time for all the niceties you're used to. When we see something we want, we go straight for it."

"But you couldn't want me! You've only known me a few days!"

Will's voice was serious. "I never knew how much I could want something until you looked up at me in the parlor where I set you down the night you came."

His burning eyes pierced through her.

"You have to be joking. The audacity —" She invented anger to account for the hard beating of her heart. "What makes you think I could ever marry an Arizona cowboy?"

He smiled, the last thing she had expected. "How about a North Carolina cowboy? Arizona is my adopted state."

"So this is the famous southern charm and courtesy I've heard about!" Her sarcasm brought another grin. Was the man *enjoying* this skirmish? She felt herself blushing again.

"Well, let me tell you, Mr. North Carolina-Arizona, when I marry someone it will be because I love him, not just for the sake of convenience."

"Glad to hear it." He picked up his hat and smiled a curious smile, his eyes glinting through the semi-darkness like the eyes of a cat. He stepped down the porch stairs until his eyes were on a level with hers.

"Shall I tell you about yourself, Miss Cartwright? You're an eastern gal who came out to Arizona with all kinds of ideas stuffed in her head. You've read books showin' how glamorous life is out here. You've visualized cowhands spendin' most of their time strummin' guitars and doing trick-ridin' on their horses.

"I'm sorry, more than I can ever tell you, for what you've been through. But it can't be changed. You can't go back. You've got to meet Arizona like it is. There's romance, sure, but this is a hard land, sometimes even cruel. It takes strong people to survive. The beauty is a wild beauty, the people plain and simple.

"If you want to ever find happiness here, you'll have to change yourself. You can't change Arizona. You may be able to help those you teach. But you're going to learn more than you ever thought. Are you a big

76

enough person for that?

"I s'pose, according to your eastern customs, it was an insult for me to speak out and tell you you could always marry me. But it's not an insult out here. It's about the highest honor you could be paid. And I won't be the last to ask. I'd bet my favorite horse, Apple Pie, against anything you want that before one month has passed, you'll get at least half a dozen proposals — and they won't all be as respectful as mine."

His slow drawl stirred her. On impulse, she held out her hand before he could turn away into the darkness.

"I'm sorry I was angry, Mr. Clark — Will. It's just that —" Her voice trembled. "As you said, everything is so different from what I had expected."

Will stood with his hat still in his hand. His face brightened.

"I know you've had a lot to face. And it isn't over yet." His hand pressed hers, then let it drop. The devil-may-care gleam came back to his eyes.

"Don't forget, Miss Cartwright. When you get all those proposals I talked about, my offer still stands."

He stepped away from the porch, then softly called back over his shoulder.

"Remember, I asked first." Only a slight

rustling in the trees showed where he had gone. Angela stood open-mouthed, staring off into the darkness after him.

Chapter 6

It didn't seem fair for the sun to shine so brilliantly during Abe's burial. Angela stood close to Mom Olson and listened to the words of the simple backwoods preacher. She had been amazed at how many of the nearby ranchers and townsfolk left their work and chores to come and honor her brother. He must have been loved.

She caught glimpses of school children peeking from behind their mothers' skirts, and a pang went through her. They were Abe's children — his students. A great longing began to grow within. She would take Abe's place, study if she had to, and help these children the way he had done.

When the service was over, Will Clark helped Angela into the buckboard. Shielding her from curious eyes, he stood before her, hat in hand. He looked unfamiliar in his plain, dark suit.

"I reckon Abe would have been proud of you," he said.

A warm glow replaced the solid knot that grief and loneliness had woven inside Angela. She couldn't speak, but he seemed to understand.

"Take her home, Owlhoot." He was still standing there, bareheaded, when they drove away.

The long stretches of silence between Angela and the Olsons were broken only by Owlhoot's sharp commands to his team. But as they rounded the last bend before reaching the Double O, Angela spoke.

"Mr. Olson?" She caught the involuntary wrinkle of his nose. "I mean, Owlhoot. Do you think I could have Abe's job?"

His astonishment showed that Mom hadn't mentioned anything to him. He grinned broadly.

"Why, I don't see why not. You've had schoolin', anyone can see that. No reason why you couldn't do a fine job." His hearty approval was just what she needed.

"I'll drop by and see Doc Bennett and Denham, maybe this evening. They'll be tickled to think we've got us a schoolmarm so easy."

"You really think I can handle it?"

"Shore." His eyes traveled up and down her slight frame. "You got that same sparkle Abe had, and you're a whole lot prettier."

Angela laughed aloud. "You do wonders for my morale!"

"It's all true," Mom Olson said. "The only young-uns you might have trouble with are the Siller boys. They haven't had much bringing up."

She saw the frown on Angela's face and added hastily, "There, don't you go worrying too much. If they don't behave, you don't have to keep them in school. They're the only two big boys — they'll stand taller than you. They aren't far in school. I think Abe said they'd missed. Anyway, you'll only have through sixth grade this year."

"Yes, that's a relief! I don't know if my mathematics is strong enough for the higher grades."

Owlhoot grinned again. "Better study this winter. You'll have to face it next year if not this."

He reined in the team. "Whoa, there! Can't you ornery cusses see we're home?"

Home! Angela looked at the sprawling ranch house. The late afternoon sun dappled the porch where she and Will had talked the night before. On impulse, she asked, "Is it true the cowboys, the young men out here — I mean, will they come see me?"

"Will they!" Owlhoot chuckled and Mom laughed out loud. "You'll have so many proposals you'll lose count!"

Angela's face flushed, remembering what Will had told her. How much else of what he

81

had said was true?

Mrs. Olson shot her a keen glance. "I guess you'll be able to hold your own. Any boyfriends back home?"

"None who will be following me." Owlhoot caught the bitterness in her voice, but decided to ignore it.

"Good. You'll want to marry a westerner, when you get ready to settle down. Now, take young Will Clark. He's a right up-and-comin' young man. A girl could do a lot worse than to pick Will Clark."

Angela opened her mouth to deny her intentions of *picking* anyone, but the humor of the situation struck her. If only Owlhoot knew of Will's early bid for her attention! She managed to answer demurely enough, but her twinkling eyes gave her away.

"Mr. Clark is a nice man. Of course, I haven't met all the others yet."

Owlhoot's answer was short. "You won't find one better than Will." He leaped from the buckboard and helped the women down, then climbed back aboard and headed for the barn.

"Oh, dear, I'm afraid I've offended him." Angela started after him, but Mrs. Olson stopped her.

"Don't worry about it. He just can't stand anyone not worshipping Will Clark the way he does. Will's the closest thing to a son we've ever had." She smiled.

"Not to matchmake, but Owlhoot's right — a girl could go a lot farther and do a lot worse!"

The door banged behind her, and Angela leaned against the porch post, laughing. They'd have her married off in spite of herself if she didn't watch out!

Her eyes crept to the small log cabin a little way from the bunkhouse. In spite of herself, a smile crossed her face. What would it be like to be married to Will Clark, to live in that primitive cabin as his wife? Her face flamed. Why had her heart taken a giant leap when she thought of it?

"Stop it, Angela Cartwright," she ordered herself, but it was no use. Suddenly she was consumed with a burning curiosity to see the inside of that cabin.

Peering both ways to make sure no one was watching her, Angela ran lightly to the cabin. It was larger than it had looked from the ranch-house porch. The peeled logs were fitted snugly together to protect against the cold. Why, there were even red-checked curtains at the tiny windows. Mrs. Olson must have made them.

Heart pounding, Angela tapped on the door, knowing Will was not at home. She slipped inside — and stopped short.

Will Clark was standing across the room. For one moment, Angela thought she would curl up in a heap of embarrassment.

"What are you doing here?" she cried out in surprise.

Will raised his large innocent eyes to meet her gaze. "I live here, ma'am."

Angela hated herself for the flush she knew was flooding her face. She had made herself look ridiculous. She must say something, explain her presence. But she was too surprised to speak.

"Come in, ma'am." Will started toward her across the spotless board floor. "Might as well get the lay of the land."

With nameless sound, Angela fled. Peals of laughter rang in her ears. That insufferable man was laughing at her! Why had she ever thought he was nice? He was odious, conceited, arrogant. Imagine telling her she had come to get the lay of the land, almost as if he expected her to be moving in with him! The thought only deepened her color. Why *had* she gone to his cabin?

Angry tears burned in her eyes, leaving them more brilliant than usual. She couldn't go back to the ranch house, not like this. Blindly, she took a little-used path back of the cabin, running under the Ponderosa pines, putting as much distance between herself and that wretched man as possible.

Angela ran for what seemed like miles until she stumbled over a fallen log. The country was far more wooded than the ranch. Thank heavens she had stayed on a trail — at least she could find her way back when she chose to go.

But how could she ever face Will Clark? What must he think, finding her stealing into his cabin when he was supposed to be gone?

"Who cares what he thinks!"

"Ma'am?"

Angela whirled, her hand to her heart. Had he followed her? No, this man had red hair and a wide grin. He must be one of the Double O hands.

"Anything I can do to help?" Something in his eyes flickered. "It's all right. I'm Red Taggart. Saw you coming through the trees and thought you might need help. Looked like you had up a pretty good head of steam." His laugh was as infuriating as Will's.

She turned her back on him. There was something about him she disliked, distrusted. "Thank you. But I prefer to be alone."

"All right with me, ma'am." He walked past her to a horse that stood nearby. "Good night, miss." He touched his wide hat and swung easily into the saddle.

"Good night." She couldn't help admiring his grace and the clean lines of his horse. Only one thing marked the smooth side of the sleek animal — an odd mark — OO.

Angela's stomach churned. She had seen that mark before. Something about it summoned unpleasantness. She sank to the ground against a huge tree trunk and closed her eyes. Why should that OO mark leave her shaken and frightened? It was a brand, she knew that. Well, of course! It must be the Double O brand that belonged to the Olson ranch.

Suddenly, Angela's face blanched, and there was a flair of recognition. *That same mark had been on the side of the horse carrying the rider who shot at her in the stagecoach.*

"Oh, no!" Her cry was a stifled whisper. It all came back at once — the horse with its brand, the rider deliberately taking aim, the shots, the plunge over the cliff. Her enemy was someone from the Double O ranch!

Angela sprang to her feet, terrified. What if it were that red-haired rider? She must get back to the ranch. Turning, she fled down the forested path back the way she had come, expecting every moment to hear the pounding of hooves behind her.

Even if it wasn't Red Taggart, someone on the ranch was her deadly enemy, someone on the ranch where she had felt safe. She must tell Owlhoot and Will and — she stopped in mid-stride.

"I can't tell anyone. What if it's one of them?"

It was out in the open, the lurking fear that had gripped her ever since seeing that brand on Red Taggart's horse. What if Will Clark . . . She couldn't finish the thought. No! Every beat of her heart denied the charge.

Still, Will had known she was coming. Abe had trusted him, told him. Was that why Will had been so kind? Was it just a trick to win her trust?

Shaking, Angela suppressed a small scream. It couldn't be true. Yet, Will Clark had laughed and told her he was *staking his claim,* getting his bid in first. Suppose he had known there was gold. Suppose he had failed to find it in Abe's cabin. There was another way to get that gold — marry Abe's sister, the sole heir to the fortune.

"No, no, no!" Standing stockstill in the middle of the path, she forced herself to face her suspicions. Who would be in a better position to benefit than Will Clark? But if she couldn't trust him, how could she stay on the Double O, even until the fall school term began? She couldn't. She must plan, get away. What should she do first?

Shadows lengthened as she tried to think. At last, she came up with a plan. By the time she reached the clearing by the ranch house, it was almost pitch dark.

"Angela!" A deep voice came from the shadows, then strong arms held her close for a moment. "Are you all right?"

Angela's heart leaped in response. It was Will! He had been worried about her. He couldn't be guilty! Then she forced herself to step back. Of course, he would pretend concern.

"I'm quite all right, thank you." She surprised herself with the coldness of her tone. Will shook her slightly.

"Miss Cartwright, it's dangerous in this country, especially after dark."

"Yes, isn't it?" She wrenched free. "I stayed longer than I intended. Good night, Mr. Clark."

She maintained her dignity and crossed the yard to the house, leaving him staring after her the way he had done the night before.

"You all right, miss?" Owlhoot's worried face peered at her from the front door. "Will's been out of his head worryin'."

Again Angela's heart leaped.

"Has he? How kind."

The temptation to confide in Owlhoot faded. He would never believe anything bad about Will Clark.

"Child, you mustn't wander around after dark." Mrs. Olson's face was grave. She had shooed Angela upstairs and then brought her a supper tray.

"I didn't mean to go so far or stay so late. I had things to think about." At least that was true. Emboldened, she continued. "Mom, don't think I'm ungrateful, but I was wondering how soon I could get settled in Abe's cabin?" She ignored the wary, hurt look in the older woman's eyes.

"I'd like to get all settled in and studied up so I can do a good job." A new thought struck her, leaving her wide-eyed. "I am going to get the job, am I not?"

"You have it. Owlhoot rode into town and talked with Doc Bennett and Denham. The job's yours — with one request."

Angela held her breath. "One request?"

Mom Olson avoided looking directly at her. "We all know you've been through a difficult time and everything, but the men

89

think it'd be better if you didn't wear black in the schoolroom. Our children have a hard time of it, and —"

"Folks won't think badly of me?"

"Of course not, child. Just wear something simple. Don't you have some other dresses in that big trunk?"

Angela sprang to life.

"Yes, I do." She slowly lifted several dresses out, one by one, remnants of a different way of life. "But maybe they're too gaudy."

"They're sure not what Broken Rail's used to," Mrs. Olson said, and held up a scarlet party dress edged with tiny, black ruffles.

" 'Bout the only women who wear red out here are, well, not our kind."

Angela delved deeper into the trunk.

"I think —" She tossed out several dresses. "Will these do?" One was a rich, dark green with piping. Another was deep blue with a tiny white collar. The third was a soft gray, edged with lace. "They're the simplest I have, and I don't have money for others."

"Land sakes but I never saw such dresses!" Mrs. Olson said. "They'll be fine. A mite more dressy than we're used to, but serviceable and neat."

She reached for a white dress with frills and flounces. "You can be married in this one."

Angela didn't tell her that the last time she had worn that dress she had gone dancing with Captain Forbes. Instead, she carelessly stuffed it back in her trunk. "That won't be for quite awhile."

"How come all of a sudden you want to get to town? Thought you was going to stay with us until fall."

Angela blushed. "I just think it's better this way."

"Whatever you say," Mom Olson sighed. "I'd hoped to have a gal around for awhile." She slipped quietly out of the room.

Angela wished passionately that she could throw her arms around the motherly woman and explain everything to her. But she couldn't. Slowly, she put the dresses back in her trunk. She had delayed unpacking until after the funeral. Now, when she unpacked, it would be in Abe's little cabin.

The next morning, Angela decided that she couldn't stand the black gown she had been wearing any longer. Instead, she donned a simple gingham house dress that she had bought to wear at the shore. If she was going to be wearing color, why not start now? As she started downstairs, she could hear Owlhoot and Mrs. Olson talking. She paused a moment and listened.

"Still don't see why she's so all-fired anxious to move," Owlhoot grumbled.

Holding her breath, uncertain as to what to do, Angela continued to listen as Mrs. Olson's voice floated from the kitchen.

"Let her go, Owlhoot. There's more to this than what it 'pears to be. I saw her talking with Will, then she came in all red and fussed. Probably some kind of quarrel. We have to let her go."

"Don't see why she should quarrel with Will. She barely knows him." Angela detected a little resentment in Owlhoot's reply.

"What's more important is that he knows her," declared Mrs. Olson. "He's been half crazy about her ever since Abe showed him her picture and said she was comin'."

"Will? Hard to believe," declared Owlhoot. "He told me there was a girl back home in North Carolina who turned him down. He didn't reckon he'd ever look at another gal."

"Well, he's looked at this one. Far's I can see, she's got him wrapped around her little finger and don't know it."

Angela crouched on the stairs. She hesitated for another moment, then, determined to hear no more, she called out gaily, "Anyone up?" and ran down the rest of the stairs to the kitchen.

Owlhoot's smile warmed her through and through. He might not approve of her criticizing Will in any way, but he still liked her.

"I'm hungry as a bear," she confessed.

"Better lookin' than any bear I ever saw," Mrs. Olson smiled. "Good to see you in something besides black."

Angela's lips quivered. "You said not to wear it, and —"

"That's right," Owlhoot said. "You know, Abe wouldn't want you to grieve over him too long. Sure, you'll miss him, but you're young and have life ahead. Don't waste the present livin' in the past."

Angela blinked as Owlhoot's kind hand touched her shoulder on his way out. She turned to his wife.

"Did you tell him I'd like to get settled in town?" she said, pretending that she hadn't heard their conversation.

"He said we can go in today and see about it. The sheriff will have had the cabin cleaned and Abe's things packed. It shouldn't be much of a job to get the place ready."

"I can have my first lesson in cleaning," Angela said cheerily, forcing back the shadow of Abe's name. Owlhoot was right. There was no use living in the past that couldn't be changed.

By late afternoon, the little log cabin had been cleaned inside and out. Mrs. Olson had even found time to pull a few weeds from the tiny flower bed in front of the weathered logs.

On their way home, Mom Olson sighed. "It's ready. You can move in any time you want. Sure will miss you. How am I going to teach you to cook and sew, with you livin' in town?"

"I'm sorry, Mom," Angela said sincerely. "But I think this will be for the best. You showed me how to use the stove, and you said you'd give me some written-out recipes. I'll be all right."

"If you're bound and determined to go, and I know you are, we might as well take you in tomorrow," Mom continued. "But I sure hate to think what Will will say when he gets back and finds you gone. He's out with the boys looking for the ornery skunks who've been rustlin' our cattle and who killed Laramie and probably Abe."

She glanced at Angela. " 'Pears to me Will's taken a powerful interest in you since you came."

Angela's heart began to pound at the

mention of Will's name.

"I'm sure Mr. Clark has plenty to do without concerning himself over me.

"Look, Mom," she said, then, deliberately changing the subject. She pointed to a giant red outcropping of rock, reared against the blue sky.

"I'll never get used to this country."

"I think you will, child," said Mrs. Olson with a quiet smile. "I think you're going to find your place is right here in Arizona."

Chapter 7

The red-circled date on Angela's calendar seemed to blink at her with a knowing eye from its place on the rough log wall of her new home. September first. The first day of school. The date was rushing toward her at lightning speed.

"I can't understand where the summer has gone," she confessed to Mrs. Olson on one of the ranch woman's infrequent visits to town. "I've studied and studied since Melissa sent the books she had been storing for me. But I still don't know if I can handle my teaching job."

"You'll handle it." Mom Olson looked around the tiny cabin with approval. "Look at the way you jumped in and made this old cabin into a real home."

The wave of her hand indicated white curtains, crooked stitches and all, a few pictures — even a drinking glass filled with now-wilting wildflowers.

"How's the cooking coming?"

Angela grimaced. "I thought fine — until I made my first pie. I buried it in the back yard."

"Buried it!" Mrs. Olson burst out laughing.

"I wasn't going to let anyone know I'd turned out such a monstrosity." Angela giggled like a small child.

"First, I forgot that you knead bread dough and just roll pie crust lightly. By the time I got through kneading the crust and baking it, it looked like a slab of cottonwood.

"Then, I forgot to turn it to keep it away from the hot side of the oven. The berries boiled over and I had a mess, in more ways than one!"

She held out her hands, no longer white and useless. A long red streak ran across the top of one.

"Souvenir of my black beast," she said, pointing to the stove.

Mrs. Olson put her arm around Angela's shoulders. "Child, you'll do just fine!" she beamed. Her spontaneous approval meant a great deal to Angela. In spite of the laughter, it hadn't been easy.

"I'm determined to make it," she said, firmly.

"And you will," Mom promised. Then, looking around the room with forced nonchalance, she asked, "How's everything in the beau department?"

"Beau? Oh, you mean gentlemen callers?" Angela's laugh this time rang out freely.

"Well, if I didn't know I'm one of the few young women in this part of Arizona, I'm sure my head would be turned!

"In the weeks I've been here, every cowboy from the Double O — well, almost every cowboy — has been here with a message from you that you wonder how I am. Have you really been inquiring after my health and welfare so often?"

"Of course not!" The hearty answer brought a dimple to Angela's cheek.

"I thought not. They have those big innocent eyes and act so serious." She mimicked a drawling cowboy to perfection.

" 'Jest tho't I'd drop by and see how ya'll are. Mom Olson'll be wanting to know.' " Her rosy face sparkled with fun.

"I can't help liking them. They're just big boys in spite of those awful guns they carry!"

"Who else has been here? Any of the townsfolk?"

"Any!" Angela groaned. "All of the single men! Even old Mr. Beale dropped by to say he calculated as how I might need a protector in this wild and foreign land. He said he'd be proud to have me think of him as my father."

"That old goat!" Mrs. Olson snorted. "He's been trying to marry every gal that's come to town for the past thirty years!"

Angela laughed and continued. "Then there's Mr. Denham from the hotel. He dropped some pretty broad hints that he's looking for a mother for his two boys who'll be in my school. Thank heavens Doc Bennett's happily married, or I suppose he'd be over, too. What makes them all come? I know I'm new and everything, but it's really getting ridiculous."

Mrs. Olson looked at the fresh face, then responded with an understanding tone, "I reckon they just like to come." But irresistably, her curiosity got the better of her. "How are you handling them?"

Angela sighed. "Well, I told Mr. Beale that his offer was just wonderful. I said that my own father would rest easier knowing that someone was looking after me. He left smiling and assured me that he meant what he said, but he hasn't been back since, thank goodness.

"After the third time Mr. Denham came, I had to tell him that I was too immature to even consider taking on the job of mother as well as teacher.

"I said, 'Mr. Denham, you know what? You need a real mature lady, one who could provide those boys of yours with a lot of guidance. I was talking with Mrs. Bartlett just the other day, and do you know how much she admires you? Why, she said she thought you were doing a grand job raising those two boys.

" 'She also said she had been so lonely since her husband died, trying to make a little money by sewing, she didn't know what to do. She certainly thinks you are a fine man.' " Angela's dimple flashed again.

"Well, now," said Mrs. Olson, "I wondered when I saw Mr. Denham come into church last week with Mrs. Bartlett on his arm. So you had something to do with it."

Mrs. Olson's face reflected the fun in Angela's. She was beginning to believe Angela could certainly take care of herself. But Angela really hadn't said anything about the cowboys. "How're you gettin' along with the cowboys?"

"I'm not so sure. They're such a handsome bunch of devils, even the ugly ones! Slim and Red Taggart are the worst. I finally told them as innocently as I could that I didn't see how they could be catching any rustlers when they were here so much." A frown crossed her face.

"I don't want to get a bad name from having too many callers. With this nice weather I've managed to visit outside, but I don't know what I'll do when cold weather comes."

It was Mrs. Olson's turn to throw back her head and laugh. "Maybe by then you'll have picked one of them and the others can leave you alone. You could always tell them you're engaged. Oh, by the way," she remarked, a shade too casually, "does Will Clark ever drop by?"

"No." Angela jumped up. "Mrs. Olson, I have something for you." She ran across the room, but not before Mrs. Olson's keen eyes caught the blush that flooded Angela's ivory throat and face.

"I found this extra pincushion in my trunk. Maybe you'd like to have it."

Mrs. Olson heaved herself from the low chair she'd been occupying. "Why, I'd love it. My old pincushion's so full of holes it looks like it's been used for target practice."

"Thanks for coming." Angela hugged her. "School starts next week and I needed your visit." Something in her touch told Mom Olson that, in spite of all the visitors, the girl had been lonely.

"When are you comin' out to the ranch for a visit?"

"I don't know." Shadows filled her blue eyes like a cloud crossing the sun.

"Well, whenever you want to, just send word by one of those ornery cowpunchers.

You know the ones who are supposed to be my messengers!"

"I will."

Angela walked to the door with Mrs. Olson.

"Oh, wait! I needed to ask you something. Do you think the people would mind if I started a Sunday school for the children? Our minister only has time for the afternoon service on Sundays, since we share him with Outlaw Junction. I was wondering if the children might not like to have something of their own."

She was unprepared for the tears she saw gathering in Mrs. Olson's eyes.

"Child, that would be a mighty fine thing to do. Talk to Parson Riley about it when he comes."

"I will. I thought I could maybe tell a Bible story and sing a little. That's one thing I can do — sing. I see how hard it is for the children to sit still during the sermons. If they knew they had something special, just for them, they could do better, I think."

"You're going to prove to be our good angel, aren't you?"

Mrs. Olson didn't wait for an answer, but patted Angela's hand as she left. She gathered up the reins and turned the buckboard. Then she called back, "Don't forget — we want you to come see us when you can. So long, Angel!"

Angela laughed and waved, secure in her friendship with Mrs. Olson.

Encouraged by the woman's reaction, Angela sought out Parson Riley the next Sunday.

"I wouldn't want to interfere with the preaching service in any way," she told him. "It would be clearly understood this is not a substitute. I thought if folks were in town anyway for church, maybe they wouldn't mind staying a little longer. They could visit while the children had their Sunday school."

"Don't count on it."

Angela looked at Parson Riley in surprise. Had she offended him by suggesting such a thing? His white hair and blue eyes shone in the sunlight of the school yard.

Seeing her inquiring gaze, he grinned. "If you hold a Sunday school, I can bet most of the folks'll stay right there and listen."

Angela's eyes opened wide in horror. "You mean — grownups?"

"Grownups."

"But I can't teach grownups!" Her panic was evident. "I just wanted to have a Bible story and a few songs for the children!"

The rough hand that was so used to ministering to the old and sick gently grasped Angela's arm.

"Miss Cartwright, you go ahead and tell your stories and sing your songs with our little ones. Just don't be surprised if you have some 'big children' who hang around the back and listen."

Angela didn't have time to worry about Sunday school — the regular school was due to open in just a week. She used every waking moment preparing lessons, planning, and cleaning the little schoolhouse. Then, bright and early on Monday morning, she opened the schoolhouse door.

The classroom shone from the scrubbing she had given it. An old flag hung in the corner. On the desk lay the Bible she would use for opening exercises. The benches were lined up in rows. A big fruit jar held a bouquet of bright flowers, and a few treasured pictures hung on the walls. The school was as ready as she could make it.

"I will not be afraid," she told the potbellied stove, cold now, waiting its turn when the weather changed.

Promptly at eight o'clock, her first pupils, Obadiah and Jedediah Siller, arrived. These were the two boys that the Olsons had described as possible troublemakers. Angela set out to conquer the boys before the others came. Her smile was friendly and disarming as she held out a hand to each.

"I'm glad you've come! You know, we want to study other things than reading, 'riting, and 'rithmetic this year."

The boys faces were expressionless.

"The Olsons tell me none of the boys around Broken Rail can play a harmonica the way you two can. Did you happen to bring your harmonica with you?"

Obadiah, seventeen and the leader, stared at her, then at his year-younger brother.

"Why — no. We never played no harmonica in school before."

"Well, we're going to this year. We're going to see if we can't get some music going — maybe even put on some kind of program for all the folks," she promised recklessly. She was rewarded by a glow of interest in the dull eyes.

Jedediah eyed her suspiciously then relaxed. "We could brung 'em tomorrer."

Angela stifled the impulse to correct his grammar and smiled again.

"Good! We'll be counting on you. In the meantime, would one of you want to use mine, just for today?" She held out a harmonica that made their eyes gleam.

"Boy, what a purty one!" With a grimy hand, Obadiah grabbed it. His fingers caressed the scrollwork on the case. "I'd give anythin' to have one like that."

At that moment, Angela became determined to see that each of the Siller boys get a harmonica. But she said nothing.

"Do you think you could accompany us as we sing this morning? I want to start every day with a song."

"*I* can play," said Obadiah. He raised his hands, cradling the harmonica. The notes were astonishingly clear and sweet.

"Beautiful! Thanks, Obadiah. Jedediah, will you bring your harmonica tomorrow?"

She saw storm signals of envy and longing in the boy's eyes. "Wait, why don't you use my harmonica tomorrow? That will give you each a chance to try it. Then you can bring your own the next day."

"We will."

Jedediah's small smile faded.

"Miss Cartwright —"

Angela's heart thumped. Both the boys were a good five inches taller than she.

"Yes?"

"Nobody calls us Obadiah and Jedediah. We're just plain Obe and Jed."

Angela hadn't realized she had been holding her breath until she finally sighed in relief.

"Oh, that's fine. Obe and Jed it will be."

She wrote their names in a clear hand across a page in the book on her desk.

"Now if you'll take the back seats, I believe the others will be here soon." As she stepped outside to ring the big bell, she caught a mutter.

"She's gonna be all right — fer a gal!"

It was all Angela could do to hide her smile. She hadn't won the battle, but the skirmish had proved successful.

The rest of the children all rushed in at once. At first, they were noisy, but when they saw the Siller boys sitting quietly in the back row, they dropped promptly into their seats.

"Good morning, students." Angela's heart thumped as she faced them. There were eight in all, a small class this year. She breathed a prayer of thanks — she could have had fifteen or twenty! Then she began to call out names, sorting the children into grades and seats by age and size.

"Obe and Jed Siller — sixth grade."

"Here."

"Billy Denham."

A freckle-faced fifth grader answered, and she put him in front of the Sillers.

"Abby Bennett. Carrie Bennett."

Two giggling twins settled into the fourth-grade section.

"Betsy Taylor." A hush settled over the room as the lone third grader walked silently to her place. Angela was surprised by the girl's beauty. Her long dark hair was neatly braided, framing her dark eyes.

"I don't think I've met your folks yet, Betsy."

The child didn't answer, but one of the Bennett twins volunteered, "She ain't got no folks. She lives at the Broken Dollar."

"Broken Dollar? But isn't that —" Angela caught the agony in the girl's beautiful eyes before her long lashes hid them.

"Yeah. The saloon. She's a saloon kid," the other twin said, scornfully.

Angela was furious. "That's quite enough!" Her sharp voice effectively silenced the talebearer. "In this school it doesn't matter who folks are, or if we even have folks." She swallowed hard.

"I don't have any folks anymore, either. What's important is how much we learn." She deliberately went on with her roll call.

"Joey Denham?" Joey was a replica of his fifth-grade brother, except for two missing teeth. He smiled up at her as he settled in the lone second-grade seat.

"And we have one first grader this year — Daisy Brooks." A tiny, scrubbed face peeked up through fat fingers hiding her from 'teacher.' Angela gave her a special smile.

"It's always nice to have a first grader," said Angela reassuringly.

She turned to the class. "Shouldn't there be more students? I thought my broth— Mr. Cartwright had thirteen."

Billy Denham's hand waved wildly. "Two families moved out to Outlaw Junction. They took five kids between 'em."

"Thanks, Billy. I guess we're all here, then." She closed her roll book with a snap. This was the crucial moment. She picked up the Bible and opened it to her carefully selected first reading.

"I will read from II Timothy, 2:15. 'Study to show thyself approved unto God, a workman that needeth not to be ashamed, rightly dividing the word of truth.' " Her voice trembled a bit as she closed the Bible.

"Let us pray. Father, we thank thee for this day and its beauty. We thank thee for this country and for these students. Teach us all what we need to learn. Amen."

Angela ignored the surprise in the faces watching her. They were probably used to longer readings.

"This morning, Oba— Obe will play while we sing. Every day, a different student may choose our song. We'll learn a lot of new songs that way. What song would you like to sing, Obe?"

He didn't hesitate.

"Do you know *Bar'bra Allen*?" Without waiting, he swung into the ballad. Luckily, Angela knew it. Her clear voice picked up the melody. She was soon joined by the piping treble of the little ones and the older boys' off-key bass.

Every day, the class sang a different song, some unknown to Angela. In turn, she taught the children songs they hadn't heard. She was overjoyed to discover real talent among her students.

"We will certainly have a program," she promised, "perhaps at Christmas."

The week sped by. She found that the only time her students were likely to look for mischief was when lessons became slow or dull. To offset those times, she took the students outside during nice weather. She read to them under a big cottonwood tree in the warm afternoons when daily lessons were done.

On Friday night, she waved good-bye to the last of her students and closed the schoolroom door. Suddenly, she was tired. It had been a good week, but a hard one for a girl who had never held a job before.

"Of all the tenderfeet, I am the worst,"

110

she laughed ruefully. "But how I love them! Every one of those children — especially Betsy Taylor."

A frown crossed her face. Betsy was the only child who had not opened up to Angela. She had stumbled through her lessons in a low voice, as if ashamed to speak out. Yet she seemed to be a bright little girl.

Once in awhile, when she forgot herself, Betsy's voice rang high and clear in the group singing. Her shyness and her beauty had made her one of Angela's favorites.

Angela smoothed her hair and walked down the long, dusty street to the Broken Dollar. Intent on her concern for Betsy, she never thought of what the town's reaction would be until she opened the swinging doors and walked in.

"Why, Miss Cartwright!" The shocked voice of the bartender froze every man in the saloon. Fortunately, the usual Friday night crowd had not yet come in from the range. But the few loungers at the tables sat bolt upright.

The impact of what she was doing finally hit Angela when she saw the shocked looks on the men's faces. But she wouldn't turn back now.

"Mr. Bronson," she approached the bar. "I've come about Betsy."

"Please, Miss Cartwright." He pulled off his apron. "You shouldn't be in here." He ushered her back out the door to the sidewalk.

"You shouldn't even be talking to me. If the ladies of this town see you talking with Sam Bronson, there'll be the devil to pay." He was hurrying her along as fast as they could go.

"Stop, Mr. Bronson!" She pulled free. "I have to talk with you. Hang the ladies and anyone else who misunderstands!" Her choice of words made his mouth drop under his moustache.

"I'll come straight to the point. Betsy shouldn't be living in the back of a saloon."

The man's shoulders fell.

"I know. Her mother danced for us — Lily was a good girl. It was the only way she could make a living. I let her keep the kid with her. She didn't have anywhere else to go. When Lily died, no one wanted Betsy."

Angela impulsively put her hand on his.

"I think you're a good man, Mr. Bronson, even if you do run a saloon!" How her values had changed in the short time since she had come to Arizona!

"If I can find a real home for Betsy, will you let her go?"

"Of course. The saloon's no place for her

— but because of who her mother was, no one wants her."

"Then they ought to be ashamed!" Restrained fury flew from Angela's darkening eyes. Sam Bronson couldn't conceal his admiration.

"By George, I'll bet if anyone can shame this town into taking Betsy, you're the one to do it! I heard how folks around hereabouts are sayin' you're an angel." He caught Angela's start of surprise and nodded.

"That's right. Kids are coming home telling how they can hardly wait to get back to school. You're just like your brother."

"Thank you, Mr. Bronson. But it doesn't take an angel just to do a little kindness, does it?"

"Maybe not. But you'd be surprised to see how many times that same milk of human kindness turns sour." He cleared his throat. "I hope you can find Betsy a home."

"Good-bye, Mr. Bronson. I'll let you know."

He looked both ways to make sure they were unobserved before taking her hand.

"You know, we could get hitched and make a home for the kid." Before she could answer, he grinned. "Just funnin', Miss Cartwright. I hope you can help Betsy."

All day Saturday, while cleaning and preparing for the next week, Angela thought of Betsy and Mr. Bronson — and herself. How strange to find such caring in one she had been taught to despise! In the east, a saloon keeper counted for little in society. Yet in Sam Bronson, she had found the same kindness the Olsons possessed.

How could she find a place for Betsy? Mrs. Olson would take her, but there would be the problem of bringing her into town for school, especially during the winter. Should she take Betsy herself? She shook her head. It would never do. The town wouldn't understand.

Dispirited, Angela was reluctant to plan her first Sunday school meeting. What could she tell the children that would also hold interest for the adults who might stay? Should she just do as the Parson had said — go ahead with the little ones and let the others listen as they chose?

Halfheartedly, Angela took down her Bible. She would find a story — one the children in Broken Rail could understand. A twinkle came to her eyes. What if she were to find a parable and put it in everyday words for them?

Her fingers raced. So the grownups were going to listen. Good! They'd hear something worth listening to! Her fingers slowed and stopped at the story of the Good Samaritan. She reread it slowly. What did these children know or care about Samaritans, priests, Levites?

Snatching pen, ink, and paper, Angela feverishly filled sheet after sheet, sometimes chuckling to herself. When she was done, she squinted to read her words. Lighting her lamp, she considered what she had written. If the townspeople did not accept it in the spirit it was given, it might be her first and last Sunday school — and the end of her short teaching career!

For one sobering moment, Angela considered tossing the whole thing into the stove and starting a fire for supper. But halfway to the stove, with the pages in her hand, Angela envisioned Betsy, her midnight-black eyes filled with agony at being called a "saloon kid." Angela smoothed the pages and neatly placed them in her Bible. She could not disappoint Betsy Taylor, even if it meant losing her job.

Chapter 8

It happened exactly as Parson Riley had predicted. After he finished his sermon, he announced, "Our new teacher, Miss Cartwright, has kindly offered to have a short Sunday school for the children each week following preaching service. After the final hymn and prayer, will all those who are interested please remain in their places." The song was sung, the prayer was said.

No one budged.

Mrs. Olson grinned at Angela as Parson Riley said again, "The children may stay for Sunday school."

No one moved. Then Owlhoot, stiff in his Sunday clothes, stood up.

"Reckon if it's all the same to Miss Cartwright, we'll jest sit in and listen."

Angela was prepared. She rose and said, as coolly as if her hands weren't trembling, "That will be fine but I should warn you — this service is for the children." She smiled and gestured toward the children.

"Will you all please come closer to the front?" She was relieved to see that Betsy Taylor wasn't there.

Soon the children had assembled in a

semicircle around Angela. The curious adults filled the back rows. Angela had been amused the first Sunday she was in Broken Rail. Back home church hadn't been anything special. Sometimes she attended, more often, not. But in Broken Rail, folks drove from miles around for the afternoon preaching service.

Part of it was Parson Riley. He talked to the people, his people, like a friend, presenting God as someone who cared about Broken Rail, Arizona, as well as the rest of the world. Angela hoped his attitude would pave the way for her little parable.

"Children, most of us know the story of the Good Samaritan. Remember, Samaritans were looked down upon. Even the Jews hated them. But when a certain lawyer came and asked what to do in order to have eternal life —"

Angela saw an uncertainty in the children's eyes.

"Eternal life means to live forever. Jesus told the lawyer he must love God and love his neighbor. The lawyer thought he would trick Jesus, so he asked, 'Just who is my neighbor?' "

"What did Jesus say?" asked little Daisy Brooks. Her interest was reflected in everyone's eyes.

"He told them a story instead of answering. He told them that, once upon a time, as a man traveled along the highway, robbers took his clothes and hurt him and left him to die. A priest came past, but he didn't want to get mixed up in the man's trouble, so he crossed the road and walked down the other side.

"A Levite, who was an important person in those days, also saw the man lying there hurt. But he crossed the road, too, and didn't stop to help."

Angela could see the children holding their breath, waiting to hear what would come next.

"Then along came a Samaritan. Remember, he was considered no good, kind of like we might think of a cattle rustler these days. But he felt sorry for the poor, hurt man. He helped him and bandaged him. He even put him on a horse and took him to the nearest inn. He gave the innkeeper money to take care of the injured man.

"Then Jesus said, 'Which of these three really was a neighbor to the poor, hurt man?' "

"The Samaritan!" The children's voices rose in a chorus, and Billy Denham added, "Boy, I'd of liked to a-been there. I'd a' helped that feller."

It was the opening Angela had hoped for. Glancing quickly around to make sure they were all listening, she took in a deep breath. She could sense the interest of the adults in back, but resolutely kept her eyes on the children.

"Sometimes it's easier to understand if we see the same things happening right where we live. Billy, I believe you would have helped the man. Do you know there is a Good Samaritan right here in Broken Rail?"

A gasp from the children and round-eyed stares warmed Angela's voice.

"Yes, we have a Good Samaritan right here in Broken Rail. Can any of you guess who it might be?"

"Parson Riley?"

"Doc Bennett?"

"Mrs. Olson?"

The answers came thick and fast until Angela laughed and held up her hands.

"My, it seems we have a lot of Good Samaritans here! But the one I'm thinking of is Mr. Sam Bronson, who owns the Broken Dollar Saloon."

This time the gasp did not come from the children. Angela could feel icy disapproval from the back of the room. It didn't slow her down.

"How can Sam Bronson be a Good Samaritan? He owns a saloon!" Billy Denham said scornfully.

"Remember, Jesus told the lawyer to love his neighbor, and the Samaritan was the only one who acted like a real neighbor."

"Yeah, but how come Sam Bronson's a Good Samaritan?"

Angela leaned forward, her eyes fixed directly on Billy.

"A few years ago, a young woman came to Broken Rail, Billy. Her name was Lily. She had a little girl, and her husband was dead. There was no work for her, so she got a job dancing at the Broken Dollar. It was the only way she could make money to buy her little girl something to eat and wear.

"Not too many months ago, Lily died." The room was so quiet that Angela might as well have been alone.

"But the little girl didn't die. She was alive, and she needed someone to take care of her."

Angela paused. This was the part she must handle carefully. She didn't want to condemn anyone, yet she must make her point.

"Mr. Bronson asked around, looking for a home for the little girl. It seemed that all of them either had children of their own or they lived so far from town that it would have been hard to get the little girl into school. Some of the people didn't want to get mixed up with her because her mother had danced in a saloon."

"Just like those fellers in the story." This time it was Joey Denham who supplied the exact words Angela needed.

"Mr. Bronson didn't want a little girl to look after. He knew a saloon was no place to bring up a child. But he couldn't find a home for her. He thought about sending her to a children's home, but when he went and looked one over, he just couldn't do it. He wouldn't let the little girl go away to such a drab, dreary place!"

"So he kept her!" Joey said.

"Yes, Joey, he kept her. He feeds her and clothes her and takes care of her as best he can, even though he knows it isn't a good place for her."

Daisy Brooks put her fingers over her face again. The other children looked solemn. But Billy Denham's face broke open in a big smile.

"Then, Mr. Bronson really *is* a Good Samaritan."

"Yes."

"And if someone else in Broken Rail took the little girl, they'd be Good Samaritans, too, wouldn't they?"

This time Angela looked toward the back of the room, noting the varying expressions on the faces of the grownups.

"Yes, Billy. They certainly would be." Before he could say more, she clapped her hands together.

"Now, what hymns do you like best?" In the confusion and singing, the tension that had filled the room subsided.

Angela wasn't prepared for what followed. In her wildest imagination, she hadn't guessed how much impact the story would make on the children. The minute the songs were finished, Joey Denham ran to his father.

"Pa, why can't we be Good Americans and take care of the little girl —" He spun back toward Angela. "It's Betsy, ain't it?"

He barely waited for her nod before asking again, his treble voice loud in the still room. "Can we, Pa?"

Mr. Denham's face dropped. He looked at Joey dancing up and down.

"Why, a gal needs a woman to take care of her." As if awakening from a daze, he turned to Widow Bartlett next to him. "Miss Bartlett, would you have me and my boys — and the little gal?"

Angela saw color brightening the woman's sallow cheeks. Mrs. Bartlett was almost pretty! She had always seemed so quiet, so unsure of herself. Now there was nothing unsure in her answer.

"I'd be proud, Hiriam."

Hiriam! The folks looked at each other. He had always been just "Denham" to them!

Mr. Denham grinned. "Well, then, any reason why we can't get hitched next Sunday when Parson Riley comes back?"

"Whatever you say." Angela caught the fondness in Mrs. Bartlett's eyes.

"We're goin' to be good Americans! We're goin' to be good Americans!" Joey Denham sang.

"Samaritans," Billy said, "not Americans."

"Same thing — hey, that means we got a sister!" For a moment the prospect of being a good Samaritan dimmed. "She won't boss me around, will she?"

" 'Course not," Billy said, with all the assurance of a fifth grader. "She's a gal, and we gotta take care of her."

The first Sunday school in Broken Rail broke up on a wave of laughter. When everyone had gone except the Olsons, Owlhoot approached Angela.

"That was a mighty fine thing you did, young lady."

She faced him squarely. "I didn't know if I should, but when I thought of little Betsy —"

"Child, you're earning your name. You've been an angel ever since you came here. An Arizona angel."

"I agree." Mr. Bronson's voice came from the doorway. How had he heard about the meeting so soon? He gripped her hand tightly in his.

"I never thought of myself as one of those Good whatever-they-are. But I thank you, on behalf of Betsy."

School had been peaceful the first week, but it was even more so the second. The minute Angela's opening exercises were over on Monday morning, Joey Denham wildly waved his hand.

"Miss Cartwright, Miss Cartwright!"

"Yes, Joey?"

He jumped up and faced the class, his missing teeth leaving a wide gap in his big grin.

"I just have to tell that Miss Bartlett's a-marryin' my Pa, and Betsy's goin' to be our sister and we're goin' to be good Americans."

"Samaritans," Angela corrected.

"Yeah, that too." He sat down abruptly.

It was Billy's turn. He stood up, belligerence in every inch.

"Joey's right." He impaled the Bennett twins with a glance. "And if anyone has anythin' to say about it, it'd better be good." With another warning glance, he sat down, leaving two half-frightened twin girls huddled in their seats.

"Oh, and yer all invited to the marryin'." Joey wasn't to be cheated out of the last word. "Pa says since we're gettin' two women the same day, we'd better make it a real party."

A real party, Angela thought as she sat with Mrs. Olson later that week. The wedding was the first social event to be held since Angela had arrived.

"Will folks think it strange if I go? With Abe, and everything."

"They'd think it all-fired stranger if you didn't go. You put on that pretty blue dress with that white stuff at the neck and don't worry over what folks think." She chuckled, the creases in her face deepening.

"Not that I can see you've been overly careful to worry about what folks say so far!" She leaned back and grinned.

"Why, I hear tell you were a-holdin' hands with the bartender right in broad daylight in the middle of the street for the whole town to see. 'Course, it was for a good reason, seein' you were sweet-talkin' Sam Bronson into lettin' Betsy stay with proper folks and all."

She broke off, alarmed at the look on Angela's face. "Why, child, I thought you'd think it was funny."

"Funny? To be gossiped about like that?"

"Sure, you're a marked woman, Angela. This old town had been settled back in the dust a long time. Then you come along like a fresh breeze and stir things up. Why, folks are bound to talk."

"What else are they saying?"

"Why, just that your comin' is the best thing that's happened around here for quite a spell."

Angela relaxed. "Then it's all right. I was afraid folks might think I'd interfered and not want me to keep teaching." Her voice trembled. "Mom, you can't know how much I'm learning to love these kids."

"Don't be too sure about that. It shows in the children."

Angela carried her blue dress to Mrs. Bartlett's for mending. She was surprised to see that the home was almost bare. Hiriam Denham had already moved most of Mrs. Bartlett's things to his own big home in back of his hotel.

"Miss Cartwright, I'm so glad you've come. I need your advice." Mrs. Bartlett laid a heavy black dress on her bed. "Should I wear the white collar with it, or just the cameo brooch?"

Angela looked at the dark dress — the same one Mrs. Bartlett had worn every Sunday since Angela had known her.

"Wouldn't you like to wear something different to be married in?"

Shame colored the woman's thin cheeks. "It's all I have. I reckon Hiriam would give me money to get somethin' else, but I want to go to him in my own clothes. Time enough for him to be a-buyin' for me after we're married."

She fingered the black material. "I did look in the store but all they had was more black and cotton. If I'd had material, I could have sewed somethin'."

Angela suddenly grabbed Mrs. Bartlett's hand. "Come on! We don't have any time to waste." She pulled the woman out the door and down the street, ignoring Mrs. Bartlett's protests. They flew past the doctor's office, past the hotel, to the school and the little attached house.

"There!" Angela threw wide the door, raced across the room, and pulled back the curtain that served as her closet door.

"You're just about my size. You can have anything you want."

"Miss Cartwright!" Mrs. Bartlett stared as if Angela had taken leave of her senses. "Your beautiful dresses? I couldn't!"

"Of course you could." Angela was determined.

"I'll never wear out all those dresses. They're all I have left from back east, and most of them aren't even practical out here."

She pulled them forward one by one, a cream with wide collar, a dark green, a gray, a maroon. Dress after dress was stroked and admired. Angela could see how starved this little seamstress was for something beautiful of her own! It must have been heartbreaking for her to work on other people's clothes and never have anything but the plainest for her own wardrobe.

"Which one do you want?"

"If you really mean it, could I have the cream-colored one?"

"Of course, but try it on first. It may not fit as well as the others." Angela was right. The dress was too long for Mrs. Bartlett, and the color didn't suit her complexion.

"I reckon I could hem it, but somehow it just don't suit," Mrs. Bartlett sighed. Angela held up a soft, well-cut, blue dress.

"Try this, Mrs. Bartlett."

The woman turned to the mirror and smiled. "Why, I look real nice!"

Angela couldn't help but hug her. "You do indeed! Would you like to take it for your wedding dress?"

Mrs. Bartlett's eyes glistened.

"I'd be proud." She fussed with the lace collar. "Why, it comes right off! How handy. Then, when it gets dirty, I won't have to wash the whole dress. And I could wear the dress on Sundays, and put on the collar for weddin's and such." She was still chattering as Angela folded the dress and wrapped it in brown paper.

"It's my wedding gift to you, Mrs. Bartlett. Your wedding gift to me is much greater — giving Betsy a home."

For a moment, the two women were no longer teacher and widow, but neighbors who shared a common concern, a little girl who had not found life an easy place.

"Miss Cartwright, I'll be thankin' you."

"I'm glad I had something to give." Angela knew she had found another staunch friend, and not just because of the dress.

Saturday afternoon, some of the school children gathered at the schoolhouse. Under Angela's instruction, they moved benches against the walls to clear a place for the wedding. Then they gathered flowers and orange-gold leaves.

"Everyone's comin', Miss Cartwright," Billy Denham said, his cheeks pink from polishing windows. "The whole Double O's comin' and the Bar Q, and the Coffeepot Slash and —"

The mention of the Double O caused Angela's heart to pound. Would Will Clark be at the wedding?

Wearing a soft yellow dress, her red-gold hair caught back with a brown velvet band, Angela attended the "marryin' party." Accustomed to pomp and ceremony, she was amazed at the simple way Parson Riley called Mrs. Bartlett and Mr. Denham forward at the end of his sermon.

He hesitated, then said, "And since this is going to be the joining of a family, will William and Joseph Denham and Betsy Taylor come forward?"

Only wide-eyed stares met his request until Angela prompted in a low tone, "Billy — Joey — Betsy, that's you."

The three children moved near the couple, and Angela blinked back tears. Just before Parson Riley pronounced them man and wife, Betsy leaned slightly against Mrs.

Bartlett, who automatically put her arm around the beautiful child in a simple white dress and held her close. Betsy had found a home with a real mother.

"Thanks, Miss Cartwright." A whisper came from behind Angela. She turned in time to see Sam Bronson scuttling out the door.

"Wait, Mr. Bronson," she said as she slipped out the door behind him. "Thank you for getting that beautiful dress for Betsy."

"Reckon it was the least I could do," he said gruffly, but Angela could sense the softness behind his words.

"Mr. Bronson, you really are a good Samaritan — and Betsy won't forget it."

The forlorn look in the man's eyes lifted. "I have to get going." He walked away, but the soft look in his eyes stayed with Angela long after he had gone.

"Good afternoon, ma'am." Angela whirled to find Will Clark standing behind her. There were sun sparkles in his blue eyes and his carefully combed hair. He looked handsome, but uncomfortable, in his dress clothes, and there was something disturbing in his glance.

"Why, hello, Mr. Clark. How nice that you could get in for the big event."

"Always have had a hankerin' to go to weddin's. This one was nice. But then, I've seen all kinds. And in every one of 'em, the bride and groom seem to have the same look I saw on these folks' faces today."

"Really, Mr. Clark, are you some kind of authority on weddings? With your interest, I'm surprised you haven't had one of your own."

Will raised one eyebrow. "I'm working on it, ma'am. Yes, you might just say I'm working on it."

Angela hated herself for the flood of color in her face.

"Oh? How interesting," she sniffed, but her tone proclaimed it was anything but.

Will took one step closer and looked down at her. "You look mighty pretty in that dress. The gals out here don't wear dresses like that much. The women don't wear ones like Mrs. Bartlett was married in, either. I wonder where she got it?" His keen eyes bored into her. "I guess I don't have to ask."

Furious with him and herself for the way her unruly heart was acting, she swept past him.

"Really, Mr. Clark," she sounded like a parrot repeating herself, "I must go in now."

"Sure, Angel."

"What did you call me?" She whirled around, almost bumping into him.

His air of innocence didn't falter. "Angel. That's what all the folks around are calling you. An-ge-la is too hard. We never knew any gal named that. Now Angel is a lot easier, a whole lot."

Why, the man was positively garrulous! Angela couldn't help staring.

"I never knew angels wore yellow. Thought they'd wear white. You got a white dress, Angel?" The corners of his mouth tipped up until he looked like a cherub. "Gals wear white dresses when they get married. If you don't have one, better be gettin' one."

"I don't see why it should concern you, Mr. Clark. I'm not planning to be married for some time — if ever."

He didn't move a muscle. "Now, beggin' your pardon, but folks' plans get changed a lot out here. I've been fixing up my cabin and all. You can do your part by getting that dress ready." He flashed his maddening grin, clapped on his sombrero, and backed away, still watching her.

"Long courtships are frowned on in Broken Rail. The sooner folks get hitched, the better. Good-bye, Angel — for now."

Chapter 9

It was long after midnight when Angela awoke. She had tossed and turned, haunted by devilish blue eyes and a southern drawl repeating over and over, "Better get ready." Finally, she had dropped into a restless sleep only to be disturbed by — what? Clutching the bedclothes closer, she lay wide-eyed in the darkness. She had heard a sound. Was someone in her little cabin?

Before she could move, she heard it again — a scraping sound. Forcing herself to open her eyes, she stared into the room. Empty. The pale moon outlined the entire cabin. Waves of fear washed over her. For these past weeks, she had been so busy with her school and the wedding that she had almost forgotten the danger.

Now it all came back — the shots and the runaway stagecoach. The torn-up cabin and Abe's murder. Her clothing strewn about at the bottom of the cliff. Should she call out, awaken the closest neighbors? They would be glad to come over. But what was there to find?

She slipped from bed and, with trembling fingers, lit her lamp. The little cabin was as cozy as ever. Perhaps she had imagined the sounds. Yet it was a long time before she slept again.

Angela's eyes were heavy when she opened the door to the schoolhouse the next morning. She had lain awake for hours, tensely waiting for the next sound. The first streaks of dawn had painted the sky before she fell asleep.

"Miss Cartwright!"

Angela turned from the half-open school door to see Obe and Jed Siller running down the trail, their smiles wide.

"We came early, like you told us, so we could larn some more 'bout that new song you was teachin' us."

Angela sighed. Would she ever be able to teach the boys proper grammar?

"Come in and we'll go over it. Oh, I'll have to run back and get my harmonica."

She ran lightly through the covered porch to her cabin, snatched up the harmonica, and was back in a moment to find the two boys staring open-mouthed at the blackboard.

"Whatever —" Her voice died. In letters a foot high, crudely printed and sinister, was a warning.

IF YOU WANT TO LIVE, GIT OUT OF BROKEN RAIL. Angela's first thought was that one of the Siller boys had played a trick on her while she was getting the harmonica. Indignant, she started to accuse them, but quickly stopped herself. Surveying the schoolroom, she realized that the boys couldn't have done all this damage, not in the few moments she had been gone.

Benches were overturned. Every drawer of her desk had been emptied upside down onto the floor. The contents had been scattered as if someone had frantically pawed through them. The flag was torn from the wall and crumpled into a heap on the table. Books were thrown about. The potbellied stove stood open, its door sagging on its hinges and ashes everywhere. Evidently, the intruder's search had been thorough.

"Miss Cartwright —" Obe Siller swallowed hard. "I'll git the sheriff." She could hear his boot heels· pounding across the little wooden porch, then up the dusty road.

"Who could-a done it?"

"I don't know, Jed," Angela shivered. "I thought I heard someone in the night, but this!" She dropped weakly into a chair.

"Someone doesn't want me here." She clenched her hands to hide their shaking.

"Me 'n' Obe'll look after you." For just an instant, Jed's rough hand touched her own.

"Thank you, Jed." The warmth of her

voice made him blush.

"What's the trouble here?"

The sheriff stepped in, followed by Obe. He surveyed the room with eagle eyes, then turned to Obe at the sound of childish voices from outside.

"You there, Siller, keep all the others out. No need to git them all upset."

Obe stepped outside and closed the door. Angela could hear him telling the others there'd been someone in the school and class would start late. The next moment he was back inside.

"Now, who found this?" asked the sheriff.

Angela started to speak, but Obe beat her to it. "We did, Jed 'n' me."

"How'd that happen?"

Angela guessed that the sheriff had the same suspicion she'd had earlier, that the Sillers were up to no-good. With difficulty, she found her voice.

"I told them to come early. We're working on a song. I opened the door, but then remembered I'd left my harmonica in my cabin. I ran to get it. I wasn't gone more than a minute or two. When I got back, the boys were staring at the board."

Suspicion faded from the sheriff's eyes. "Miss Cartwright, did you see or hear anything at all, maybe in the night?"

"Yes. I woke to hear a scraping noise. At first, I thought it was in my cabin, but no one was there. I lay awake for a long time, but I didn't hear anything else."

"Did you light the lamp?"

"Yes." She didn't explain how she had lain shaking for what seemed like hours trying to get up courage to light that lamp.

"And you heard nothin' after that?"

"Nothing."

"Uh-huh. The way I figure, whoever was here saw the light and got scared off." The sheriff began combing every inch of the schoolroom. The Siller brothers followed him.

"Here!" Obe cried. He snatched something from the floor. "Why, it's —" Shock replaced the joy of discovery.

"Hand it over." The sheriff glanced down at the object. His face sagged. "I wouldn't have believed it."

"Believed what?" Angela's breath came in short gasps.

"See?" The sheriff pointed to the carved initials. RT. Following them was the familiar symbol OO.

"The Double O? RT? Red Taggart?" Angela's eyes were filled with horror. "That nice cowboy did this? Is he the one who tried to kill me — maybe even killed Abe?"

138

Her slight frame shook with disbelief.

"Sorry, ma'am. It looks that way. No other reason for Red's quirt to be here, is there?"

"Maybe from the wedding —" But Angela's fading voice denied her words. It had been several days since the wedding. The quirt would have been discovered long before this.

"Reckon I'll just have to ride out and have me a talk with Mr. Red Taggart."

"Sheriff, may I speak to you before you go," Angela asked. Then she stopped to smile at the boys. "Would you wait outside, please? I want to speak with the sheriff. Then we'll put the schoolroom back in order."

Obe and Jed silently backed out the door and closed it behind them.

"Sheriff," she said, trying to steady her voice. "I should have told you before, but it was a Double O horse I saw the day I came to Broken Rail." Her face was pale.

"Why in tarnation didn't you tell me sooner?" His question was just one shade under a roar.

"I couldn't. The Olsons had been so good to me." Her face pleaded for understanding. "I had hoped it was all over. Whoever went through my clothes didn't find

anything. I had just hoped it was all over."
Drained, she looked up at him again.

"Fool thing to do." The sheriff glared at
her. "You knew he didn't find what he
wanted — hey, just what is it he wants? Do
you know?"

"I'm terribly afraid I do." She lowered her
voice to a whisper. "Just before Abe died, he
murmured, 'Something big. Gold. I hid it.' "

"Where?" The sheriff's question cracked
like a whip.

"He didn't say. He died before he could
tell me."

It was the sheriff's turn to be shocked.
"Young lady, you should'a told me or Will
Clark or the Olsons! Do you know the
danger you're in?"

She nodded mutely as he figured out
loud.

"This gent must've got wind of the gold.
He almost certainly knew Abe mentioned it
to you." He pulled a bandana from his
pocket and mopped his face. "He ain't goin'
to stop 'til he gets it."

"Should I go away?"

"No! Don't you see, you're safer here
than if you went somewhere else. At least we
can keep an eye on you here."

He leaned toward her. "Miss Cartwright,
I asked you before and you couldn't answer,

bein' upset and all. Now I want you to tell me every detail of that first day you came to Broken Rail."

Licking her dry lips, Angela repeated everything that had happened. "I finally raised up — and saw him," she concluded. "It wasn't until later I saw the brand, the Double O on the horse."

"What color was the horse?"

Angela closed her eyes, willing herself to relive that awful moment. The masked rider, the slowly raising rifle, the brand. "A strange color — almost cinnamon-colored."

The sheriff recoiled. "Cinnamon? You mean goldy-brown?"

"Yes."

The image was coming clearer.

"With that double O on it?"

The sheriff suddenly looked older than anyone she had ever known.

"Why, Sheriff, what's the matter?"

"There's only two horses like that on the Double O."

"Whose are they?" Angela bit her lip until she could taste blood. It seemed an eternity before he answered.

"One is called Apple Pie — and belongs to Will Clark."

"Oh, no!"

"The other is named Burnt Sugar — and

Red Taggart owns him."

Angela felt torn apart. Two of the cowboys who had laughed with her, visited her, and in Will Clark's case, proposed to her.

"I can't believe it!" Her wail rose in despair. "Not one of them!"

The sheriff's face turned to granite. He pocketed the quirt as he started toward the door.

"I guess *this* tells us which one of them it is." Before she could speak, he was gone.

What seemed like hours later, Obe Siller quietly stepped inside. "You ready for us now, Miss Cartwright?"

She could see anxiety in the big boy's face. With an effort, she pulled herself together.

"Yes, Obe. Please erase the board first, then bring the others in."

All through the exclamations of surprise, the cleaning up and the belated lessons, Angela moved mechanically. Self-discipline kept her going, but her heart and mind were riding with the sheriff on his way to the Double O ranch.

"Howdy, Sheriff!"

Owlhoot's call failed to bring a reply from the tall man riding into the front yard of the Double O. Only when the sheriff dropped the reins did he return the greeting. A deep crease cut between his eyes.

"Owlhoot, I've got some mighty bad business."

"With us?" The rancher's keen eyes spotted the droop of his old friend's mouth.

"You caught one of my boys rustlin' cattle or somethin'? Wish you'd catch whoever's rustlin' *our* cattle — we lost another hundred last night."

"Last night?" The sheriff's head jerked up. "Then all of your boys were out chasin' rustlers?"

Owlhoot snorted. "Where else would they be?"

In answer the sheriff held out the quirt. "Recognize this?"

"It's Red Taggart's. Everybody knows that, you old fool."

"Then maybe you can explain how it came to be on the floor of the schoolhouse this mornin' when Miss Cartwright opened up."

The deadly seriousness of his face stilled Owlhoot's joking.

"And maybe you can explain how come there was a sign on the board tellin' Miss Cartwright to git out of Broken Rail if she wanted to live, and why the schoolhouse looked like a barroom brawl had hit it."

"You don't mean it!" Owlhoot hitched closer. "Miss Cartwright was threatened?"

"She shore was. Afraid I'm goin' to have to ask Red Taggart some questions, Owlhoot."

"But Red was with us —" He squirmed under the sheriff's questioning stare.

"At least he started out with us. You know how it is — you're all together, but in the dark and everything, it's easy to git separated."

"Sorry, Owlhoot. I've got to see him."

Owlhoot threw up his hands. "All right, but I'm tellin' you, Red Taggart just plain wouldn't do any such thing!"

"Wouldn't do what?" Red and Will Clark lazily walked toward them.

"Hey, Boss," Red complained, "if I spend many more nights in the saddle like last night, I'm goin' to ask for a job doin' dishes for Mom!"

"Red, the sheriff'd like to ask you a few questions."

"Shoot. I got nothin' to hide."

"Oh?" The sheriff held out the quirt and watched Red carefully. "This belong to you?"

A delighted smile spread across the big cowboy's face. "Hey, where'd you find that? It's been missin' for more'n a week."

"Missin', huh? Funny it should turn up in the schoolhouse." Again, the sheriff scanned Red's face. "Any idea how it got there?"

"The schoolhouse! How would it git in the schoolhouse?" Was there a trace of uneasiness in his manner?

"The schoolhouse was busted into last night, Red, and busted up 'most as bad as Abe Cartwright's cabin."

The sheriff measured the effect of his words on his listeners.

"You wouldn't know nothin' about writin' on the board warnin' Miss Cartwright to git out of Broken Rail, would you, Red?"

"Why should I?" His face flamed, eyes hard. "You sayin' I did all that?"

Will spoke for the first time, his eyes fixed on his partner.

"He's just askin', Red." He waited. Red didn't answer. Will's face set.

"Now *I'm* askin'. Do you know anything about it?"

"While you're thinkin' about it," said the sheriff, "you might also tell us why the horse bein' rode by the man who ran Miss Cartwright's stagecoach over the cliff was wearin' a Double O brand."

"That's a lie!" Red reached for his gun.

"Hold it, Red!" Will Clark stopped his

friend's quivering hand. "Sheriff, you'd better have some pretty good evidence to back that up."

"The best." The sheriff's gaze was as stony as Will's own. "Angela told me this mornin'."

"How come she never said anything to us about it all the time she was here?" Owlhoot blustered.

"I asked her just that question. She told me you'd all been so good to her, she didn't want to make trouble. She figured maybe it was over. She was hopin' the killer'd given up and moved on."

Will stepped closer to the sheriff. "What else did she say?"

The sheriff hesitated, then let them have it.

"The horse she saw, the one with the Double O brand —" He paused until Will's nerves screamed. "That horse was cinnamon-colored."

"Cinnamon-colored! But Apple Pie and Burnt Sugar are the only two saddle horses we got that answer that description," Owlhoot protested. "An' you know they belong to Will and —"

"Yeah. To me." Red dropped his bluster. "All right, Sheriff. I'll go with you if that's what you want."

"Red!" Will's voice stopped him in his tracks.

"Leave me be. If the sheriff's so all-fired anxious to arrest somebody, it might as well be me."

Will's mind was whirling. It was impossible for Red to be Abe Cartwright's cold-blooded killer. Red cared less for money than anyone on the ranch. And he was acting almost as if he were protecting someone. But who?

A wisp of memory tickled in Will's mind. The day Angela Cartwright had come to Broken Rail, something out of the ordinary had happened. What was it? Suddenly, it all came back.

"Sheriff, I don't know how Red's quirt got in the schoolhouse. I do know he couldn't have been the gent who ran the stagecoach over and tried to kill Miss Cartwright." Will leveled his voice.

"Red borrowed Apple Pie to ride into town for a wagon part." His heart sank as he remembered that Red had come back without the part.

"Apple Pie's cinnamon-colored, too."

Red laughed. "So he gets me either way." His face turned dull red again. "Thanks, Will."

The sheriff looked nonplussed. "Red, if

you can tell me fair and square you know nothing about this whole thing, I'll take your word for it."

Never had Will seen Red cooler. He shoved his big hat back. "Afraid I can't do that, Sheriff."

"Red! You're lying! You can't mean you were in on Abe's killin'?"

"No. But the way I figure it, if a man knows somethin' about a low-down skunk and doesn't do nothin' about it, ain't he guilty?"

"Then you're protecting someone."

"Not exactly." He shook his red head violently. "I just suspect somebody. I can't prove anything."

At the sight of Will and Owlhoot's shocked faces, Red relented. "Aw, guess I'll have to come clean," he said, rolling a cigarette.

"Remember when Laramie was killed? How I wouldn't believe someone in our outfit was in on that rustlin'? Well, I started watchin'. Little things started happenin'."

His usually ruddy face was shadowed.

"That day when I borrowed Apple Pie, I headed out past the range where we keep our horses. Out of habit, I looked around for Burnt Sugar. He wasn't there.

"Didn't think much of it until later. I left

Apple Pie here with you and took one of the broom tails out to git Burnt Sugar. Burnt Sugar had been rode and rode hard."

"Then you're sayin' someone borrowed your horse, met the stage, shot at Miss Cartwright, left her for dead, and returned your horse, all in the time you were gone?"

Red's eyes met the sheriff's. "Sounds purty thin, but that's how it was."

"I believe you, Red. But you ain't tellin' all you know. How about last night?"

Will could feel the air stiffen. "Answer him, Red!"

"All right." There was defiance in Red's voice. "I wrote that message on the blackboard."

"I don't believe you!" Will bellowed.

Red's voice was calm. "I can prove it. It said, 'If you want to live, git out of Broken Rail.'"

Will's troubled eyes sought out the sheriff, who shook his head regretfully. "Those were the exact words, Will."

"But why, Red?"

" 'Cause Angela ain't safe here no more. Last night, when we were a-chasin' rustlers, I noticed one of our boys broke off and headed toward Broken Rail. Since I'm naturally a curious guy, I rode after him. He swung into the trail that hits the road for town. I followed — right to the edge of the schoolhouse, but some distance back. He never knew I was there."

"And?" Will couldn't stand waiting for Red's lazy voice to continue.

"And I peeped through the window. I watched him bustin' up the place."

"Who was it?"

"I didn't see his face. All of a sudden, a light came on in Miss Cartwright's cabin. The varmint blew out his lantern and ran for the door. I waited to make sure he wasn't goin' to hurt Angel. I didn't dare follow too close. Instead, I slipped into the school. I had to warn the little schoolmarm, so I wrote the message on the board. Then I snuck out.

"When I got home, all the horses were in the corral, still warm. I slipped in the bunkhouse. All the beds were full."

"And you still don't know who it was?"

"I know," Red said with a steely voice, "but I ain't sayin' until I can prove it. Now here's my plan. Sheriff, you go ahead and run me in. Let everyone in town know you've got Abe's killer." A strange look crossed his face.

"It'll be mighty hard on the Angel, findin' out one of the cowboys she's been so nice to is guilty. But it can't be helped."

"I don't see what good runnin' you in is goin' to do," Owlhoot exploded. "How's that goin' to help us catch the killer?"

Red's eyes filled with golden flecks of light. "You and Will and the sheriff are goin' to be watchin' the Angel. You're also goin' to be watchin' this outfit to see who's sneakin' out nights."

Owlhoot scratched his head. "I don't know. When the folks around Broken Rail hear tell you killed Abe Cartwright and tried to shoot his sister, they ain't goin' to take kindly to the idea. What if they hold a hangin' party with you as the guest of honor?"

"They won't. The sheriff's goin' to let me escape soon as word gets out what a bad hombre I turned out to be."

"Oh, I am, am I?" the sheriff scowled. "I've never let a prisoner escape yet."

"Well, this'll be the first time. Once I'm free, I can find out what yellow-bellied snake is in our outfit. He won't be expectin' anything except you-all to be lookin' for me. That's when he'll go after Miss Cartwright."

Red's face gleamed. Hatred distorted the usually open features.

"And I'll be waitin' for him."

"Sheriff?" Will turned toward the

lawman. "How about it?"

The sheriff shook his head. "Mighty risky, I'd say. What if this feller we're after gets wind that it's a put-up job?"

"Then that feller has to be you or Owlhoot or me. Take your pick," Will said as he turned toward Red. "Just one thing. I'm goin' in this with you."

"You're *what?*"

"You heard me. I'll break you out of jail and the sheriff can spread the word we must have been in this together. We can't take any chances on not catchin' the skunk who's really guilty."

An approving grin crossed Red's face. "Might not be such a bad idea. Tell around town we been leadin' a double life. Just been waitin' to make a real killin' and leave the country. Why not even spread around that we're back of the Double O cattle bein' rustled?"

Owlhoot choked and a glimmer of humor shot through Will. Accused of rustling his own cattle!

"Wonder what the Angel will think of that!" Red said with an irrepressible grin. Will didn't answer. She would just have to believe what she wanted until this was all over.

Never before had Angela simply endured

the day in the classroom. But, today, every bone in her body ached from holding in the hurt and bewilderment of finding Red's quirt. It was with relief that she rang the final bell and dismissed her students. Her relief was short-lived. Not more than ten minutes after school was out, Billy Denham raced back to the school with the news.

"Miss Cartwright, Miss Cartwright!" He gasped for breath. "Sheriff and Red Taggart just rode in. Red was in handcuffs, and I heard the sheriff tell Sam Bronson that Red confessed!" The words hit Angela like a boulder.

"You mean —"

"Red killed Abe and tried to kill you and tore up the school and —" Billy stopped to swallow. "And all the time we thought he was such a good friend of yours."

"I thought so, too," was all Angela could get out, but it didn't matter. Billy was long gone, off to spread the news before someone else beat him to it.

Why had she ever come to such a terrible land? Angela fought the panic rising within her. Had she ever known a blacker moment than finding out someone she had trusted was a killer?

Answering a knock at her door the next morning, Angela faced the sheriff. His head

153

was bandaged and his eyes were dull.

"Sheriff! Come in, what happened?" She led him to a chair.

"I'm sorry to tell you this, Miss Cartwright, but Red Taggart broke jail last night. You need to be mighty careful. No tellin' what he'll do."

Angela could feel the color receding from her face. "I will."

The sheriff shook his head mournfully. "Never can tell about folks, especially folks you trust. That's only half the news. Will Clark broke him out. Didn't even bother to wear a mask. Just looked me right in the eye and said, 'I'm takin' Red.' "

He gently touched his head. "Wasn't much I could do about it."

"But why? They were good friends, but why would Will help a killer?" Angela's cry forced the sheriff's eyes away.

His mouth was grim, his lips compressed. "I'm afraid there's just one answer. Appears to me they must have been in it together, or Will wouldn't have broken Red out of jail. He must have been afraid Red would spill the beans and tell how they had planned the whole thing and killed Abe."

Chapter 10

Will Clark — a murderer! She had fallen in love with her brother's killer. Even if Red had pulled the trigger, Will was just as guilty. Angela felt dizzy. Nausea filled her. When had she learned to care about Will? The moment he set her down in the hall of the Double O? When he had been so kind during her confusion about Abe's death?

Her newly recognized love turned to ashes. With white lips, she managed to say, "Thank you for telling me, Sheriff. I'll be careful."

She saw the look in his face and knew she had given herself away. When he was gone, she sank to a chair and buried her face in her hands.

"I'll go back east," she said aloud to comfort herself. "With my teaching experience, I can surely find something to do. I can become a governess or care for children. I'll scrub floors if I have to, but I won't stay in Broken Rail."

Then practicality struck her. Until she received her first month's pay, she didn't even have train fare. Would the Olsons loan her the money? The next hours were a jumbled mass of half-plans, regret, heartbreak. So this was Arizona, the land she had longed for, the land Abe had loved and called for her to share. It had brought her nothing but misery.

"I'll go where no one has ever heard the name Cartwright. Maybe I'll take a *new* name. I won't think of all this."

It was small comfort. When her clock struck the early morning hours, Angela wearily rose and threw herself on top of her bed. Though her body was exhausted, her mind kept running like a squirrel in a cage. Some time later, she became aware of outside noises and bolted upright. This time, she did not huddle in a frightened heap in bed.

"Who's there?"

Only the night wind answered, but Angela knew some terrible evil lurked outside. How long would it be until it entered her cabin and overpowered her? She tiptoed to the window at the back of the cabin. It was small, but it would have to do.

Carrying her shoes in one hand, she gently raised the window, taking care not to make any noise. No one would ever expect her to try the window, and the log cabin only had one door. She said a quick prayer of gratitude for the darkness of the night, then lifted her long, full dress and put one leg over the sill.

What was that? Frozen in place, Angela heard the cabin door creak, then give. Someone must have slipped a knife in under the drop latch, raising it enough to open the door. With a terrible sense of urgency, she dropped the other leg over the sill and pulled her skirt with her.

She would wait until whoever it was went to the bed to find her. The bed was far from the door, so she would have a head start before the intruder could leave the cabin.

Eerie shadows swirled around her as she waited. She heard a man's rough whisper. "We've got to git her out of here, Red. We'll kidnap her and —"

Only by sheer will power did Angela control a betraying cry. She recognized the voice — it was Will Clark! For one moment of agony, she clung to the sill, then dropped lightly to the ground. Slipping from tree to tree, Angela gave thanks that she had worn a dark dress.

As she crept behind a giant clump of bushes, something touched her arm. She thought she would faint. A soft whinny almost sent her into hysteria. Horses! Could she escape on one of them?

Fumbling for the reins, Angela bundled

up her long skirts and managed to mount the horse. It whinnied again.

"Red! Someone's at the horses!" Footsteps pounded across the yard toward her. "Come on, let's go!" She dug her heels in the horse's sides, unaware that she had dropped her shoes. The soft touch of her stockinged feet was enough for the well-trained horse. As Angela gripped the reins, he sprang ahead.

Angela tried to steer him toward the sheriff's office, but the horse had other ideas. Unfamiliar with the lighter weight on his back, the gentler touch on the reins, he laid his ears back and galloped down the long, dusty street.

"Whoa, boy, whoa!" she cried. The sheriff's office flashed past.

It was no use. Angela gave up trying to stop him and just hung on. How long would she be able to stay in the saddle without being thrown?

The horse gradually slowed to a long, rhythmic stride. Angela found herself clutching the saddle horn. At least the stirrups were the right length. Suddenly, she realized why. The two men had fitted out the horse to carry their victim away. That was why he had been closer to the cabin than the other horses.

Behind her, Angela heard shouts. Once, she thought she heard a shot. Her heart nearly stopped.

"Oh, no," she cried, her words snatched from her to be lost in the road behind. "Please don't let him be killed."

She considered what Will Clark might be facing at that moment. If the townspeople caught him, they would lynch him and Red both. Strange how she couldn't grasp that he was a cold-blooded killer! All she could remember was his kindness.

About a mile out of town, Angela's horse slowed. Ahead, a crossroads shone in the pale moonlight. Angela's heart leaped to her throat.

At the crossroads, a mounted figure sat motionless, dark against the night. He was waiting.

"Go, boy!" she cried, but she was too late. The statue-like figure spurred forward, grasped the bridle of her horse, and forced him to a standstill.

"Whoa, there, Burnt Sugar! Miss Cartwright! What are you doing out here?"

She strained her eyes to see under the shadow of the man's hat brim.

"Slim! Thank goodness!" Slim would help her. "Red and Will, they've broken jail — they tried to kidnap me tonight!"

Slim was curiously still. Impatient at his lack of understanding, she cried, "It's true! They shot at me and killed Abe! I've got to get away. Will you help me?"

Finally, the cowboy was galvanized into action. "I sure will." He looked back down the empty road. "Come on! We have to git away pronto."

"I don't know if I can ride very fast. I don't have any shoes!"

He looked shocked. "You rode clear out here with no shoes?"

"I had to." Suddenly Angela was exhausted. "Can you get me to the Double O?" She could feel his stare.

"No. That's the first place they'll come. You don't think the Olsons will believe anything against Will Clark, do you? I heard Will bought into the Double O a while back." Slim's voice was hard. "Wonder if he was countin' on paying for his share with the gold your brother found and hid."

The final damning evidence set Angela reeling in the saddle. A poor cowboy would never have had money to buy into a ranch like the Olsons'.

It wasn't for another mile down the road that she regained some of her senses. "Slim, how did you know about the gold?"

"Aw," he seemed reluctant to tell her. "I

heard Red and Will talkin' —" She lost the rest.

A long time later, she asked, "Where are you taking me?"

"There's a line shack down in the canyons. No one will think of it — at least not for awhile. By then, I can git you out of there and take you some place where it's safe."

It was enough to satisfy the weary girl. She silently clung to the reins until, in a weak voice, she said, "Slim, I don't think I can hang on any longer."

Instantly, he was beside her, helping her down. "We'll ride double. You can hang on to me."

Gradually, Angela could feel that they had left the road and were starting down the canyon. They twisted and turned as the night wind cooled her burning face. By the time dawn came, she was ready to collapse. Would she awaken in her own log cabin and find it had all been a terrible nightmare?

She opened her eyes wide when the sun came up, its morning rays glistening on the heavy dew that had fallen during their ride. She had been only vaguely aware when Slim stopped earlier and wrapped something warm around her. Her feet were blocks of ice.

"Almost there," Slim assured her.

"Why, what are all those cattle doing here?" In spite of her dizziness, she was surprised by the great herd peacefully grazing in the secluded valley.

"They're drifters. When the colder weather starts, they drift down here."

Funny, she wouldn't have thought they'd drift down such a narrow, windy way as they had come, but she was too tired and stiff to care. Slim lifted her off the horse and carried her into the cabin.

"It ain't much," he apologized, dropping her onto a rude bunk, "but it's clean." He smiled at her. "I'll git a fire a-goin' and fix up some grub." He was already rummaging in the stacks of cans. "Later today, I can shoot a rabbit and get some fresh meat."

"Won't they follow us?" Angela's eyes were too heavy to stay open.

"Naw. I'll just send Burnt Sugar on his way. He'll go back to the Double O. By the time they find this place, we'll be gone. Plenty of other horses down here fer us to ride." His spurs clinked as he crossed the board floor.

Something was wrong with what he had said. Instinctively, Angela huddled against the far wall of the cabin behind the bunk. All thought of exhaustion was gone. Why should there be plenty of horses in this se-

162

cluded place? Do horses drift, the same as cattle?

She crossed the cabin, standing next to the open door but out of sight. Why did she suddenly feel in danger? Slim had been as courteous as Captain Forbes or her eastern friends would have been — and a lot more resourceful!

Peering out the open door, she saw Slim emptying the saddle bags. Had Will and Red packed them full of food? Would they have brought her to an isolated cabin such as this? For the first time, she took in her surroundings. High, red rock walls rose a thousand feet into the air. There were peaks and flat tops and a red dirt valley floor with a stream sluggishly meandering through. And there were cattle everywhere, hundreds of them!

Again, a faint warning bell tinkled in her mind. So many cattle had drifted down such a crooked trail?

Her puzzled attention turned back to Slim. He had uncinched the saddle and removed the bridle of the cinnamon-colored horse. Slapping its rump, he called out, "Git home, you Burnt Sugar!" And then, "goodbye and good riddance!"

Burnt Sugar leaped high, then galloped across the valley. But the white-faced girl in the shelter of the crude doorway choked and staggered to the bunk.

Will Clark and Red Taggart were innocent — the man who had shot at her, who had run the stagecoach over the cliff, was now in total power. It had to have been Slim. No one else on earth could reproduce those exact words in that exact tone of voice.

"Good-bye and good riddance!" Angela had run from friends playing some mysterious game — and was caught in a trap of her own making.

Angela heard Slim's slow step. She feigned sleep, steadying her breathing so her heartbeat could not be heard. Her only hope was to keep Slim from learning that she had discovered the truth. He had tried to kill her before. It would be simple enough for him to dispose of her in this faraway place.

An involuntary moan escaped from her lips. Slim crossed the cabin. It took every ounce of control she possessed not to shudder when his calloused hand touched her forehead.

"Feverish. No wonder." Slim dipped his bandana in water and bathed Angela's face. She forced herself to continue the deep, even breathing. Why was he caring for her like this? Then the truth struck her. He still believed she knew where the gold was. He had to keep her alive to find out.

Through half-closed eyes, she could see him moving around the cabin. His acting was superb. The knight preparing breakfast for the lady in distress. How could she be so ravenous when she was in danger? She must throw him off his guard, pretend to be innocent of his plans. Could she outact him? She had to.

"Slim —" She slowly opened her eyes. "I'm so tired — and hungry!"

He wheeled from the open fire in the rude fireplace. A big smile covered the lies that spread across his face.

"Why, that's fine, Miss Cartwright." He dished up something hot from the kettle. " 'Fraid it ain't the best, but it's fillin'." He brought the battered tin plate to her bunk. "Canned beans. Canned corn. There's even canned peaches for dessert."

"Thank you, Slim." She forced a smile.

He dished up a plateful for himself. Heartened by her first few bites of hot food, Angela asked, "What are we going to do? How are you going to get me out of here?"

He glanced at her and her heart lodged in her throat. Had she gone too far?

"At first, I thought we'd just ride out later today. But maybe that's not such a good idea. Why don't I go back to Broken Rail alone? Nobody will know I even saw you." His voice grew more enthusiastic.

"I can pick up that bag of gold and act real surprised about yer bein' gone." He grinned again. "Wouldn't hurt none to git you some shoes, neither."

Angela tried to act nonchalant.

"How will you get my shoes without being seen?"

"Aw, I can creep in after dark. Miss Cartwright, where's that gold hid?"

It had come, the moment she had feared. If Slim once thought she didn't know, there would be no reason for him to keep her alive.

He mistook her silence for hesitancy. "You can trust me, ma'am. You'll need the gold to git away."

"Well." She hesitated, her mind racing. He knew it wasn't hidden in the cabin or the school. *What should she say?* Frantically roaming the cabin with her eyes, she focused on a pile of firewood. Did she dare? It was the best she could do.

"Slim," she clutched the tin plate, "the bag of gold is hidden —" She saw the flare of greed in his eyes. "It's hidden beneath that big woodpile back of the school."

He expelled his breath as if he'd been

holding it. "Why, shore, that sounds right. Abe must have known Will 'n' Red would be after that gold. So he hid it in the wood-pile."

Curiosity overcame caution, and Angela leaned forward. "Slim?" she asked. "You said you overheard Red and Will talking about the gold. Just what did they say? Where did Abe find it in the first place?"

Slim took a long swallow of coffee before answering. Was it to give himself time to make up another lie? Angela's eyes never left his face.

"Seems like your brother was bit by the gold bug. Folks around Broken Rail knew all the gold had been gone a long time, but Abe liked to poke around in old buildin's. Out past Outlaw Junction, there's an old, deserted place called Minerstown. Folks say it was started up by an old prospector. One day, he came tearin' into town shoutin' that he'd found gold. But he didn't have nothin' to prove it. Or, if he did, he wouldn't show it.

"When Outlaw Junction sprung up, the few folks in Minerstown moved away. All but the old prospector. He lived in an old shack by himself. Didn't like other people. Always said he was goin' to strike it rich.

"Anyhow, Abe liked the story, and he

used to spend some time out at Minerstown. One day, he was takin' a look in a shack when he hit a rotten board and went through the floor. Underneath the floor, the ground was all hollered out. Abe found bones — and somethin' else."

"Gold!" Angela's eyes were wide.

"Yeah. A whole sackful. Enough to give a man a good start on a little spread." Slim's eyes glistened.

"But how did —" Angela caught herself from saying "you" and substituted, "how did Red and Will know all this?"

"Abe thought Red and Will were good friends, so he told Red about it. Then, when your pa and ma died, Abe sent for you. Said he was goin' to make a real home out here in Arizona for his sister."

"So that's how it happened." Angela leaned back and closed her eyes. It had to be true. "Red told Will and one of them tried to kill me. Then they tore up the cabin and killed Abe."

Slim stood up. "That's about the way of it." He whirled toward her. "Miss Cartwright, Angel, after I go git the gold —" He licked his lips. "I mean, after I git back and we ride out, why don't we get hitched?" He must have seen the shock in her face. "We'd have enough to git a spread, and you'd be safe. They'll hang Will and Red."

She started to speak, but he stopped her. "Don't say nothin' now. You probably want to think about it. I'll just ride on back into Broken Rail. When I get back, maybe you'll be done thinkin'."

She avoided looking at him to hide the anger in her eyes. If she pretended to agree, it might save her life. He'd know she had tricked him when he found there was no gold in the woodpile. But at least she would have several hours while he was gone.

"I certainly will think about it, Slim." Could she think of anything else?

"That's good enough for me, ma'am." He smiled again. "Might as well git ready and go back before anyone misses me. They all think I'm out combin' the draws for stray cattle." His admiring eyes sent shivers up her spine, but she hid her feelings. She could play this game as well as he.

"Good-bye, Slim." She waved to him as he mounted his horse.

"So long, ma'am. I'll be back as soon as I can. Then it's just ten miles out that-a-way to Outlaw Junction — and the parson!"

Angela watched him cross the valley and start the climb up the crooked clay trail. The instant he was out of sight, she ran into the cabin. Ten miles to Outlaw Junction!

Would the trail be so overgrown that she couldn't find it? She had to get away!

Could she catch one of the horses in the valley? No. It might take hours to track them down.

"What if Slim is part of a gang — and they come back?" she whispered, terror filling her heart again. "He couldn't have brought all this stock here by himself!"

She decided she would have to leave immediately. She would have to walk. She had no shoes and her stockings were in shreds, but she had no other choice.

Grimly, she surveyed the cabin for something to protect her feet from the rocks and cactus on the trail to Outlaw Junction. There was nothing suitable except an old blanket. It would do for leggings, but what about her feet? She ran outside. The saddle bags. Could she put her feet in them and tie them up with blanket strips?

Preparing for her journey seemed to take an eternity. She had found a discarded sombrero that would shield her head from the sun. She had hacked the saddle bags in two and wrapped the parts around her feet. Finally, she was ready.

Angela hobbled out the door and down the trail leading toward Outlaw Junction. The "saddle" shoes dragged at every step.

After the first hundred yards, she dropped to the ground and removed the bags. They would blister her feet within a mile. She rewrapped her feet, this time in the remnants of an old blanket, grimaced, and started again.

Chapter 11

"Burnt Sugar's gone!" Red Taggart made no effort to keep his voice down. "The Angel must have crawled out the window and got to him."

Will's mind clicked with a dozen plans. "She'll head for the sheriff's office. Come on!" They raced back of darkened dwellings toward the sheriff's office and pounded on the door.

"I'm comin'." The sheriff threw open the door, pulling up his pants at the same time. "What in tarnation — You! What're you doin' here?"

"We decided we had to get the Angel away." Will quickly sketched out how he and Red had waited until they thought she'd be asleep. "Didn't dare just knock and tell her the whole thing. I reckon she'd heard the news by now."

"Yeah." The sheriff's fumbling fingers had lit a lantern that flared briefly, then settled to a steady glow. "She took it hard."

Red made a choked sound. "What're we standin' here for? She was headed this way. Must not have been able to pull in Burnt Sugar."

"You boys go back and get your horses.

Meet me here in ten minutes. She'll ride straight for the Double O."

"And straight into danger." Will's steely eyes met those of the sheriff.

"Aw, come on, Will, we'll catch up to her before she gets anywhere near the Double O. Besides, the fellow that I suspect got sent out to comb draws. My guess is he'll circle back around and ride into town. He won't be anywhere near the Double O."

"I hope you're right." Will's voice sounded hollow, and his face was grim as they hurried back to Angela's cabin for the horses.

"This nag shore ain't Burnt Sugar," Red said. "Hey, what are these?" Red held up two dark objects. "Shoes! Angel must have dropped them when she ran off. She must be ridin' Burnt Sugar barefooted. Whew! Good thing he's gentle."

"That's why we picked him for her." Will replied curtly. "You ready?" Without waiting for an answer, he turned toward the sheriff's office.

"Will —" Something in Red's voice caught Will's full attention. "We've been partners a long time."

"So?"

"So I'm askin', as your partner, are you sweet on the Angel?"

Will stared straight ahead into the darkness as Red continued, "The reason I want to know is, I like her a lot, but she don't like me. Not like she does you."

"How do you know that?"

"Me 'n' Slim were always callin' on her, and she never once forgot to ask about you."

Something warm melted the icy knot inside Will. His voice husky, he extended out his hand toward his faithful friend.

"Put her there, Red. If she'll have me, I'll make her happy. Once I thought I was in love with a gal. I know now it wasn't any such thing."

"You do love her, don't you?" Will's fingers tightened in the handshake. "Then we've just got to find her," Red said.

"We will." The sheriff, who had been riding a few paces behind, caught up with them. "She'll be at the Double O, you wait and see."

But when they got to the ranch, the house was dark. Will dropped from the saddle even before Apple Pie had stopped. He raced to the door and banged on it. "Owlhoot! Open up."

"What in th—" A window opened overhead.

"It's me, Owlhoot."

"Will!" The window slammed and footsteps pounded down the stairs. A lamp flared and the front door flew open. "What are you doin' here at this time of night?"

"Is the Angel here?"

"Miss Cartwright? You crazy? There's school tomorrow. Why would she be here?"

"Red," Will ordered, "check the bunkhouse. Tell me who's gone."

"Right." Red whipped back out the door.

Owlhoot was rapidly losing patience. "Will you tell me what's goin' on?"

"There's the devil to pay, Owlhoot. Red and I figured we would get the Angel to some safe place before anything more happened. We went to her cabin, but she must have heard us comin'. She crawled out the window and ran off on Burnt Sugar. Sure she ain't been here?"

"I told you she wasn't!" Owlhoot's rage lessened. He could see the deep concern in his partner's face.

"He's gone." Red clumped back into the hall.

"Who's gone?" Owlhoot demanded.

"Slim." Will glanced at Red with surprise.

"Of course he's gone!" Owlhoot roared. "He's out combin' draws. He probably decided to stop at a line shack instead of ridin' in. You ain't accusin' Slim of bein' mixed up in this, are you?"

175

"That's right." Will hated to see the ashen color of Owlhoot's face. Slim had been one of the boss's favorites.

"How'd you know, Will?"

Will turned back to Red. "All the time there was somethin' that kept poundin' at me, but I didn't remember it until yesterday. Maybe I didn't want to remember it." His face was somber. "I liked Slim — didn't want to believe he was in this."

"An' what was it you remembered?" Owlhoot took a step nearer, his eyes glittering. "Maybe it ain't right after all."

"I'm afraid it is. Remember the day we were gettin' ready to take the Angel to town, and Slim busted in with the news about Abe? Remember what he said?"

"Sure. I ain't senile." Owlhoot's temper was being tested. "He said that Abe Cartwright had been shot and that Doc Bennett said he wasn't goin' to live."

"What else?" Will watched Owlhoot's eyes slowly widen.

"He said the sheriff was callin' for a posse and that Abe's cabin had been torn up bad."

"That's right."

Owlhoot's body sagged. "And there's no way he could have known all that if he hadn't been guilty. He was out on the range."

"Supposed to be out on the range," Will said. "He was there just long enough to borrow Burnt Sugar. That way if he was seen, folks would think just what the sheriff did — that it was Red.

"Slim must have been a busy hombre that day. First, he ran the stagecoach off the cliff and shot at the Angel. Then, he sneaked to town and tore up Abe's cabin. He probably thought if he came with the news, everybody would be so shocked they wouldn't think to ask how he heard."

"Wait a minute, Will," the sheriff protested. "All that didn't happen the same day. Miss Cartwright was shot at the day before she got here. Then it was the mornin' after she came that Slim brought the news, wasn't it?"

"Yeah. In the meantime, Laramie rode in with news of the cattle raid," Red added.

"You ain't sayin' Slim's rustlin' cattle from me!"

"I am." Red took a sweat-stained bandana from his pocket. "I found this poking around where we lost the cattle. It's Slim's."

"But why?" Owlhoot's face screwed up as if he would cry. "Why would he steal from the Double O?"

"The way I figure it, Slim was brandin'

mavericks on the sly — a few here and there to build him up a place of his own. Then some outfit caught him and throwed in with him. That's when the cows started disappearin' in bunches."

"Outfit! The big rustlin' outfits have been gone from these parts for years."

"I thought so too 'til I heard tell that Rags Malone'd been seen at Outlaw Junction."

"Last of the Crooked Canyon gang."

"Not quite. His sidekick Jasper was with him. They had to have an insider. Slim must be their man."

Owlhoot buried his face in his hands. "It's hard thinkin' one of the Double O boys would turn rotten."

The sorrow in his face was replaced by steel. "Well, what are we standin' here jawin' for? Red, git the boys from the bunkhouse. Tell them the truth — and tell 'em we're goin' to ride."

The man who only moments before had looked old and beaten, now was in total command, handling a crisis with confidence.

"This ain't no hangin' party, Owlhoot," the sheriff reminded him. "If we have to shoot, fine. But those that are willin' to give up will stand trial and go to jail."

"If you say so." Owlhoot headed for the

stairs, then spun around. "Ain't you forgettin' about the Angel in all this? Where is she?"

For a moment, there was silence. Red cleared his throat and shuffled. "Burnt Sugar would come home, if he was let."

"Maybe somethin' scared her on the road and she pulled off," said the sheriff, knowing it was small comfort. "Git that outfit, Red. Slim and the rustlers can wait. We've got to find Miss Cartwright."

The Double O hands met in front of the ranch house moments later. They were quiet and sullen after hearing about Slim.

"We'll split up," the sheriff ordered. "Owlhoot, you take Vaq and Swede. They're the best trackers. Soon as it's light, you go over every inch between here and town. Beat it in if you find anything."

He broke off, his eyes peering through the gloom of early morning. "Any reason for Slim to think he's suspected?" The hands all shook their heads. "His stuff still in the bunkhouse?"

"All except what he needed for yesterday," Red said.

"Red," directed the sheriff, "you and Will come with me. Slim's likely to make another try at the cabin or school. We'll be there waitin'."

Hours later, Will Clark stretched his stiff muscles. Waiting was just what they'd done. Mindful that the townsfolk still thought Will and Red were guilty of murder, the sheriff had ordered the two men to stake out the school and Angela's cabin. Before daylight, he would nail a notice on the schoolhouse door saying Miss Cartwright had been called out of town and there wouldn't be school that day.

There had been no word from Owlhoot and the rest of the outfit. Will knew that with all the riding back and forth, it would be hard to pick up Burnt Sugar's tracks. If Angela Cartwright should be killed, Will's world would end.

He closed his eyes and forced back all thought of her. Whatever lay ahead would require a steady hand.

Red crept over to Will and whispered hoarsely, "What if he doesn't come?"

"Then we'll wait some more." Will's nerves were on edge and Red's question didn't help. Red gripped Will's arm, then crept away to his place on the opposite side of the schoolhouse.

Dusk had fallen again when footsteps roused Will. He sat up straight and drew his gun. A lone figure was walking toward the school, slipping around toward the back where Red was hidden.

Fear sent Will to his feet. It was Slim! He was walking tall, even whistling a bit. For a moment, Will couldn't believe his eyes. Had they all been wrong? No, they couldn't be! Yet here was Slim, open and unconcerned.

"Howdy, Slim!" Will rounded the schoolhouse corner just as Red spoke. Slim was standing over the woodpile. Logs were scattered around him. "Lookin' for somethin'?"

Slim's face paled. "Red!" He forced a crooked grin. "What are you doin' here?"

"I might ask you the same thing."

Slim's color returned. "Miss Cartwright sent me."

Every nerve in Will's body turned to ice, but he didn't speak. Slim hadn't seen him yet.

Slim reached for his pocket and rolled a cigarette. "Me an' the Angel are goin' to git hitched."

Red's mouth dropped open. "You know," Red said with a suggestive laugh, "she's been sweet on me ever since she came to Arizona. How did you happen to get it settled? I thought she liked me!"

"Aw, Red, you know how gals are. Last night, she wanted me to come into town, but I didn't think I'd make it back from the range. She just up and headed out toward the Double O. I'd been thinkin' I hated to disappoint her, so I rode in. We met out at the crossroads. She didn't want to tell her school kids about our plans, so she had me come to git her things."

"Where'd she go?"

"Double O. Figured Mom Olson would understand how it is, her bein' married to a puncher an' all." Slim ended his story.

"Red, I sure was sorry to hear you killed Abe Cartwright. I won't let on to the Angel that I saw you tonight. You're headin' out of the country, ain't you? Not much choice after tryin' to kill the Angel."

"You lyin' skunk!"

Slim stepped back from Red. "What right you got to call me that!"

Will saw Slim's right hand drop low and stepped out with a warning. "Don't touch that gun, Slim. We know all about you and Abe Cartwright and the Crooked Canyon gang."

"Aw, I git it. You're puttin' it off on me so you can get away. Then take this!" His shot whistled between Will and Red. Both men automatically hit the ground. Slim dashed for the schoolhouse door and ran inside.

"Don't kill him unless you have to, Red! We've got to find out what he did with the

Angel." A volley of shots rang from the open door.

"I'll cover the front," Will said, "and you take the window at the back. It's so dark, it's like shootin' blind. Got a match?"

"Yeah."

"When I yell, light it and throw it in the window. Maybe it'll stay lit long enough to see where he is." Will huddled next to the open door. "Now!"

In the tiny flare of the match, the men glimpsed Slim's body huddled against a wall. Will shot at Slim's arm and heard Red shooting through the window. In turn, shots rang out toward the door and the window.

"Get down, Red!" Will's words were lost in a mighty clatter from the schoolhouse, as if Slim had run into something. Will tried to picture the room. What would have made that much noise? Had Slim lurched into the stove?

Another match flared. Slim was on the floor by the stove. Will heard Red's gun roar, then ran inside the room and laid low behind the desk.

There was a cold, menacing silence.

Was Slim dead or injured? Will wondered if he should strike a match, revealing his own position. Seconds passed, then minutes. Will reached for his matches. A scuffling sound from behind stopped him. It couldn't be Slim.

"Red?" His whisper sounded loud in the stillness.

"Yeah." A match flared, and Will heard a quick indrawn breath. "I reckon it's about all over," Red said. In the light of the burning match, Will saw Red's face, his lips set. "That last shot of mine must have got him."

"What's goin' on in here?" The sheriff stood at the door holding a lantern. "Slim?"

"Yeah, it's Slim. He's over there." Will and Red crossed to the crumpled body of the man they had bunked with, eaten with, and fought with side by side. "Makes you sick, doesn't it?"

"Is he dead?" Will knelt by the cowboy and put his ear to Slim's heart. "Not yet. Get Doc Bennett."

In the dim light, Slim's eyes opened. "The Angel —"

"Where is she?" The steel grip of Will's fingers seemed to steady Slim.

With a mighty effort, Slim said, "Canyon. Line shack. She —" His head fell back as life seeped from him.

"No need for the Doc," Will said as he slowly stood up. "What are the chances of gettin' to Hidden Canyon in the dark?"

Red ignored him. "Look!" Red's finger was pointed at the overturned stovepipe.

"So he knocked the stovepipe down. So what? Let's get out of here and find the Angel!"

"Hold it!" The sheriff crossed the room and lifted a heavy sack from the floor. "The gold?"

"Yeah." Red's laugh was bitter. "Slim found what he was lookin' for — too late." He wheeled toward the doorway. "Sheriff, you ready to ride?"

Before Red could step outside, Obe and Jed Siller burst through the door. They looked silently at Slim's body.

"He killed Abe Cartwright," Red said.

"What are you doin' here?" Will was already halfway out the door.

"We brung in Burnt Sugar."

"Burnt Sugar!" Will stared at the Siller boys, whose faces were ghastly in the light of the old lantern. "Where did you find him?"

Obe drew in a breath with a long shudder, then turned his back on the still figure by the stove. "Burnt Sugar came past our place this afternoon. Funny thing — there wasn't a saddle or bridle on him. Me 'n' Jed waited and waited but nobody come for him so we brung him in."

"He came past your place? But don't you

live clear down the trail toward Hidden Canyon?"

"Yeah. We wondered how Burnt Sugar got way out there. He was comin' up out of the canyon!"

Jed spoke for the first time. "We wondered if whoever rode down the canyon last night was ridin' Burnt Sugar."

"You heard them?"

"Yeah. Quiet kind of sounds, an' we found prints this mornin'." Jed's eyes were steady. "We jest mind our own affairs, mostly, but it shore seemed strange."

"We think Slim took Miss Cartwright down the canyon last night," Will said, noting the stricken look that passed between the brothers. "You boys willin' to show us that trail past your place? Can it be ridden in the dark?"

"Shore. A lotta cattle's been goin' down there lately," said Obe.

Will stared again. "How come you didn't tell the sheriff?"

"Why should we? The Sillers ain't known for good deeds. He might have thought we rustled 'em." Obe's face was hard.

"Pa says to keep still unless yer asked," Jed added. "So we kept still. But when we found Burnt Sugar, we shore didn't aim to git took fer horse thieves."

Will held his right hand out, first to Obe, then to Jed. "I'm askin' for your help."

"You got it." The boys ran outside. "Got a horse to spare? Reckon Red'll want Burnt Sugar."

"You go ahead and ride him," said Red firmly. Only Will knew the sacrifice Red made in turning down Burnt Sugar. "That horse knows the way better'n we do." Red's voice hardened. "Slim always checked out Hidden Valley Canyon when we combed for strays."

"Go ahead, Jed. I rode him in." Obe mounted a shaggy pony his brother held. "You don't think Miss Cartwright's hurt or anythin', do you?" asked Obe. "We seen some bad-lookin' fellows goin' up and down that trail. Suppose she runs into some of them?"

Jed's eyes glittered in the lantern light. "She's smart. She won't git taken by them."

"Yeah." Obe turned his mount around to ride out the way they had come. "Nobody can put much over on the schoolmarm."

As they rode, Jed's voice came back from out of the darkness ahead. "Will, Red, is one a' you aimin' to git hitched to Miss Cartwright?"

Red found his voice before Will. "Why d'ya ask?"

"Jest wanted to tell you, Obe's aimin' to ask her at Christmas if she ain't spoken for by then. Pa says she's got spunk, and Obe —" Jed's words were lost in a clatter of hooves. Brother Obe must have kicked Burnt Sugar in the side to quiet his brother.

Red Taggart had the last word. "I've done given up my claim, partner. Sounds like you best get in yours before Obe Siller beats you to it!"

Will could hear Red's chuckle at the thought of the schoolmarm being asked for by Obe Siller, whose pa thought she had spunk. The chuckle died away as they followed their guides toward Hidden Valley. They were almost afraid of what they might find.

Chapter 12

Angela's tattered clothing hung loosely about her as she made her way along the trail. She had torn her clothes into strips to bind the blanket pieces to her feet. The result was awkward, but the wool protected her feet from the rough trail. The trail was overgrown as she had feared.

"I wonder," she said out loud as she eyed the sluggish stream, "why couldn't I walk in the water?" She unbound the cloth from around her feet and legs and carefully hung the strips over one arm.

The reddish-brown water felt cool on her feet and ankles. It wasn't more than a foot deep. She slipped on a stone and fell, but she was undaunted. After all, the warm sun would soon dry her, and the coolness of damp clothing felt good.

She followed the stream until it began curving away from the rough trail. Then she reluctantly stepped out and wrapped the protective cloth around her feet.

Her panic had subsided, and, instead, she felt great relief. At least Will Clark and Red were not mixed up in the murder! She smiled to herself as she thought of Will.

"So he's fixing up his little cabin, aiming to get hitched!" A dimple flashed, and mischief shone in her eyes. "Well, we'll just see about that." The warm glow that was stealing over her wasn't from the sun.

"My friends back east will never believe that Angela Cartwright is planning to marry a cowboy! A North Carolina cowboy, at that!" She laughed to herself.

Suddenly, she stopped short in the trail. What if the townspeople captured Will and Red and hanged them before they found out the truth?

"Oh, no!" Her cry came through parched lips as she sped up her pace. She had to get to Outlaw Junction and find someone to help her before Will and Red were caught! She tried to run, but with her long skirts, everything was impossible.

With fumbling fingers, Angela unfastened her petticoats. One, two, three, they dropped in the trail. Then she rolled them into a ball and hid them beneath the spreading limbs of a stunted cedar.

Now she felt free. Her tattered skirt whipped her bare legs as she stumbled down the trail. The trail had grown more rocky, harder to follow without hurting her feet. Even the padding from the blanket pieces didn't help much. Gradually she slowed.

"I can't stop yet," she told herself, eyes fixed on a distant point. "I'll go to that big rock and stop for a little rest."

When she got to the rock, she simply tucked her tangled hair back under the old sombrero, then started on again. Something beat at her consciousness — something she should remember about Outlaw Junction.

"Got a dandy preacher," she remembered. "We share him with Outlaw Junction." The vision of Parson Riley's kindly face swam before her eyes. With new vigor, she quickened her pace.

Just when Angela thought she could not take another step, she came upon a crooked sign: *OUTLAW JUNCTION — 2 miles.*

Two miles! She stared in dismay, then glanced at the western sun. "If I've come eight, I can go two more," she said with determination.

She was afraid to examine her feet. They felt wet with blood, but she decided not to look. She thought if she knew what was happening, she might not be able to go on.

Finally, she topped a little rise and looked down on buildings. Outlaw Junction! Triumph rang in a great cry. Running down the crooked trail, heedless of her aching feet, Angela rounded the last bend before reaching town — and stopped short.

"Whoa, there, little lady!"

She had never seen such cruel eyes as the ones that peered at her from this twisted face. The man was first in a line of a dozen riders. Her eyes traveled from face to face, seeking a spark of kindliness. Instead, she saw only men in rough garb, their skin turned dark and leathery from the Arizona sun. In no face was there any sign of kindness. Far from it.

Angela's heart sank. It appeared that she had now met up with the very outlaws she was trying to get away from.

"Where did you git that sombrero?" The man's eyes narrowed like a cat.

"Why, I was lost. The sombrero was there, so I borrowed it." With a stroke of ingenuity she held it out. "Is it yours? I won't be needing it now that I'm almost to town."

"Haw, haw! She got one over on you, Rags!"

"Shut up!" Rags didn't see the humor. "I know where you got that sombrero. Just can't figure out why."

"I told you. I didn't have a hat, so I borrowed it."

"Mighty peculiar shoes you're wearin'."

Angela sat on a rock by the trail and tried

to smile disarmingly. "Aren't they! You see, I came away in a hurry and didn't have time to get my shoes."

"How come you were in such an all-fired hurry?"

Angela's shiver was real. "There was a man." Her mind worked like lightning. "We went for a ride. He said he'd take me to a pretty valley." A daring thought crossed her mind. "We — he said we'd come find Parson Riley and get married."

"So you're goin' to git married. Where's the happy feller?"

Angela kept her head down and twisted her fingers nervously, acting her part. "He — uh — I decided I didn't want to get married right now. He rode off. He said he'd be back later. After he was gone, the valley was scary, so I walked here."

"Wearin' the sombrero you found."

Angela couldn't fail to catch the disbelief in his voice.

"I reckon you're lyin'. Who was this feller that rode off and left you wearin' no shoes?"

"Slim — from the Double O Ranch."

Rag's eyes opened wide. "Slim? You mean Slim Radcliff?"

"Yes."

Rags spurred his horse until he was

almost on top of Angela. "Say, ain't you that Cartwright gal that came out from the east?"

"I am Angela Cartwright."

"Haw, haw!" Rags laughed rudely. "An' you're plannin' to marry Slim." He didn't wait for her answer. "Well, it just happens we're goin' into the valley to see Slim — on a business deal, you might say. Now, Slim would be mighty grateful if we was to bring his little filly back." He turned to one of his men and, through tobacco-stained, sun-split lips, said, "Jasper, bring up that extra saddle horse, so the little lady can ride with us."

Angela stood with every ounce of dignity she could muster. "Thank you, Mr. — Rags, but I couldn't do that." She smoothed her bedraggled dress. Lifting shy eyes, she tried to look totally innocent.

"I wouldn't want Slim to see me like this." She forced a laugh. "I'll just go on into Outlaw Junction and get fixed up so when Slim comes —" She laughed again, a nervous, silly giggle.

"I reckon he'll like you well enough the way you are." Rags met her nonchalance with equal coolness. "If he don't, I sure will!"

"Thank you again, but I really can't go

with you." Angela stepped briskly into the trail and around the horse.

"Git her, Jasper!"

Angela felt a sharp pain on the side of her head. She was falling. Strong arms pinned her own arms to her sides. She tried to raise her head but sank back, almost unconscious from the pain.

"Wonder if Slim's tryin' to give us the double cross?" Jasper said. "Funny he'd bring this gal into the valley."

"If he is," Rags said, "he's a dead man." Mercifully, Angela lost consciousness.

When Angela awoke, she was lying on a hard bunk. She slowly opened her eyes and looked around the cabin she had so nearly escaped. The cabin was empty, but voices came from outside. Her fingers gently rubbed a lump the size of an egg on the back of her head. The effort of even so slight a movement set it to throbbing. She lay back and listened to the voices.

"The dame still conked out?"

"Yeah. What did you hit her so hard for? Maybe she'll die on us."

"Aw, I just tapped her. She'll be all right."

Angela heard the rustle of paper. She pictured Rags and Jasper rolling cigarettes.

"Say, ain't that funny about Will Clark and Red Taggart gettin' stuck in jail for killin' Abe Cartwright and tryin' to run the little gal over a cliff!" Angela felt the deadliness of their coarse laughter.

"Sure is. An' when folks hear tell how Will's bought into the Double O, they're goin' to wonder where he got the money."

"Wonder how come he didn't shine up to the schoolmarm? She's a pretty little thing. Kind of skinny, though."

"Maybe he did. Slim said Red was always hangin' around. I got half a notion to ride off with the little gal myself."

"You? Git hitched?"

Rags' answer chilled Angela's blood. "Nobody said nothin' about gettin' hitched."

"Aw, boss, she'd just slow us down."

"Soon as we sell this bunch of cows, we'd better slow down anyhow, at least for a spell. This business of Slim and the gal don't set well with me."

"How did you find out Clark was buyin' out Owlhoot?"

"He ain't buyin' him out. Just buyin' in. That's how come that big herd of cattle got shipped in — the ones standin' over there! Slim just happened to be hangin' around under a window when they were talkin'. Will's old man kicked off back east somewhere and left him a bunch of money."

"Slim's good at listenin' at windows, ain't he?"

"Yeah, I'd just as soon git rid of him. He's done what we wanted. An' him bringin' that gal here bothers me some. I hear tell the whole town's lickin' her little boots — callin' her the Angel an' all that. They won't stand for much happenin' to her."

"Reckon she knows anythin' about why those cows are down here?"

"Naw! She's an eastern dummy, jest interested in clothes and stuff. Wonder how come she said she'd marry Slim?"

"She didn't. She said he said they'd git hitched."

"Yeah." Angela could hear the rasp of Rags' hand across his grizzled chin. "Bet if I spruce up and shaved, she'd like me a whole lot better. I might even turn respectable, Jasper! Get me a little ranch and raise a bunch of kids."

Angela felt a crazy urge to shout in unholy mirth. What would Captain Forbes think if he could see her now — supposedly engaged to one outlaw, another planning to turn respectable and marry her! Angela wondered if Rags and Jasper knew about the gold? It was obvious that they didn't trust Slim.

Some of Angela's fear had subsided when

Rags said the town wouldn't stand for anything happening to her. Did he mean that he would free her? Never. If he carried out what he had in mind, she'd be worse off than if they killed her.

I'll never let him ride off with me alone. Better to die fighting than be packed off by this animal.

"Hey, hadn't we better be wakin' up the gal?"

"Let her be!" Rags' command was curt. "When she wakes up she'll be askin' a bunch of questions."

"Yeah. This way, the boys can have that herd moved out before she starts to wonder about 'em." His laugh was hollow. "Pretty clever, hidin' the openin' into the cottonwoods with brush. She'll never know there's a good trail to Minerstown."

"Yeah, an' nobody goes to Minerstown. With this bunch of cows, we got enough for a big drive to Tuttle's. He don't ask no questions."

Angela heard Rags' spurs clink.

"Wonder how come Slim don't come."

"He won't git in 'til after dark, you can bet on it. He'd be scared to prowl around the school in the daytime. An' you can bet he's finishin' up the job he started the other night. How come he didn't stick it out and git the gold when he had the chance?"

"Saw a light go on in the gal's cabin and heard somethin' outside," Rags snorted. "He's about as brave as a gopher. C'mon, let's see how the boys are doin'."

Angela's muscles were taut. She was in far greater danger than before. She must get away, but how? There was no window in this cabin — only the gaping front door. She didn't even have a weapon. Was there anything in the cabin that could serve?

With courage born of desperation, she flashed across the room, ignoring the aching in her head. She held her breath as she passed the open door, then grabbed the sturdiest stick on the woodpile. Then she crept back to the bunk, hiding the stick beneath the folds of her torn skirt.

"Please, God, just give me a chance!" The silent prayer, coupled with her weapon, sent strength through her badly strained body. Even her headache lost its sharpness and became a dull throb.

Rags and Jasper were gone a long time. She had almost dozed when she heard voices. Immediately, she was alert, fingers clutching her stout weapon.

"Go see about some fresh water, will you?" Rags said. "I ain't much of a cook, but Buck's still helpin' with that last bunch of cows. I'll see what I can find inside."

Angela's heart leaped. This was it, the chance she had prayed for! With two of them in the cabin, she had no hope, but with only Rags —

"Hey, ain't you awake yet?"

She could feel Rag's hot breath as he leaned over her. Forcing herself to lay still, she waited. Closer and closer he came, until his face was only inches from her own. Was he going to kiss her? She controlled a shudder, raised her club, and brought it down on his head. He crumpled without a sound.

Had she killed him? She didn't wait to find out. Footsteps were nearing the cabin door. She snatched the pistol from Rags' belt and cocked it. Then she aimed it squarely at the open door.

"Rags —" Jasper's voice broke off in shock. "Miss —" His eyes were wide open. "You killed him!" The bucket of water he carried crashed to the floor as he automatically started to draw.

"*Stop right there!*" Her command halted his clawlike hands in midair. "If you move even one muscle I'll kill you!"

A sardonic grin crossed his face. "Now, a purty little thing like you wouldn't —"

Her gun crashed, neatly sending his hat

spinning. His face turned dirty white. "I reckon you would."

Angela could have scoffed at the awe-struck look on his face. "Now, unbuckle that gun belt and throw it at my feet — and don't try anything."

For one moment, the defiant eyes met hers, then his hands slowly crept toward his gunbelt. She raised the pistol until it was on a level with his staring eyes. There were beads of sweat on Jasper's brow as he slowly unbuckled the belt and tossed it toward her.

Holding the gun steady, she picked up Jasper's weapon and wrapped it in the fold of her dress. "Now get over to that bunk and lie down."

This time there was no argument. Jasper took one more look into the barrel of Rags' gun and eased over to the bunk. Angela backed around the cabin until she was near the door.

"I wouldn't try to follow if I were you. This gun seems to have a hair trigger."

She glanced outside, rejoicing in the evening shadows. The next moment she was out, dropping into place the heavy bar used to keep marauding animals out of the line shack. She crept step by cautious step around the cabin. There was no movement from inside, but how long would Jasper wait?

Turning, holding the gun in front of her, Angela fled into the welcome night.

Chapter 13

Angela's heart raced as she ran from the ramshackle structure now serving as a temporary jail for her captives. In moments, Jasper would raise a cry for the rest of the outfit. What would they expect her to do now that she was free?

A smile quivered on Angela's lips, as she remembered Rags' opinion of her intelligence. An eastern dummy interested in clothes. He might have been right when she lived back east. But this Arizona land had changed her.

Angela closed her eyes, putting herself in their places. Jasper and Rags would find some way to get out of the cabin, or else the outfit would be riding in soon. Suppose she were Rags? She could almost see the sneer on his face and hear his command, "Go get the little rabbit, running for her life." Her lips curved in satisfaction. After her performance with the pistol, Jasper would likely warn, "Watch your step — she can shoot."

If they expected her to run, she would do just the opposite. There was still enough pale light filtering through the tall trees around the shack for her to see she couldn't huddle near the cabin. She would be seen. Casting a suspicious eye at the biggest of the trees, she wondered if she could climb it. She swept the rest of the area with a glance, immediately rejecting any other plan. The tree was her only hope.

Silent as a shadow, she slipped to the big tree, touched it and felt oozing pitch. Good! She could cling to the sticky trunk and lift herself high into the branches and out of sight.

A nervous laugh threatened to choke her as she tucked the remains of her skirt high into her waistband. If only Rags could see her now! He wouldn't think she was such a dummy. First, her petticoats, now her skirt — what would she have to do next? Would she have to spend the night in the tree? What would happen when Slim came?

Angela refused to think about it. She safely swung herself up to the tallest limb she dared reach, then pressed against the trunk, merging into the shadows. From here she could see a bit of the cabin, but not the door. Her perch was not uncomfortable. One gnarled branch had grown crooked, in the shape of a seat. Panting, she sank back gratefully.

The climb hadn't been easy with a pistol in her hand. Cautiously, she reached in the bosom of her dress and drew out the gun she had taken from Jasper. Good! It was fully loaded. She frowned at Rags' gun. How could she use two weapons? But the danger filling the night was so strong that she dared not stash one gun in the tree. Keeping the loaded revolver in her lap, she stuffed Rags' gun back into her dress.

Suddenly, she heard a shout from below. She peered down through the heavy branches, but could see nothing.

"Hey, you ornery cowpokes, git up here and let us out!"

Angela had to press both hands over her mouth to keep from laughing. Jasper certainly wasn't in a very good mood! She waited. Jasper shouted again, and this time there was an answering "halloo" in the distance, followed by the pounding of many hooves. The outfit must have finished sorting the cattle.

Angela picked up her weapon from her lap and held it firmly as the riders swept up to the cabin. She could feel sweat breaking out beneath her dress. Could she shoot, even kill, if she had to? Every teaching she had ever known rose in protest. *Thou Shalt Not Kill.* Yet the fierceness of this country called something from inside that she hadn't known she possessed — the strong and undeniable feeling of self-preservation.

Feeling sick, she leaned back against the tree. "No! Even to save my own life, I can't do it." Nervous fingers dropped the gun into her lap.

The next instant, a small cry rose to her lips. She had just remembered Red and Will. White-faced and shaken, Angela realized that she must escape and explain everything to the sheriff and townspeople. Otherwise, Red and Will would be hanged. Perhaps she couldn't kill to save herself, but she could do it to protect the man she loved.

Angela again became aware of what was happening below. Jasper was loose. She could hear his voice. He was almost directly under her.

"That spitfire hit the boss with a stick and knocked him out, the little she-devil!"

Angela sensed admiration mixed with his rage.

"Had the nerve to hold me up with his gun. Pete, give me one of yours!"

"I always told you to carry two."

"Oh, shut up and find the gal! She can't have got very far, and if she ain't back by the time the boss wakes up —" The menace in his voice sent shivers through Angela. The men mounted their horses.

"Not even a decent rest," one of them

complained. Jasper growled something inaudible and went back in the cabin. Angela could hear him clearly. "Wake up, boss! We're in a mess!"

The outfit must have split up, Angela decided. She could still see the dark shadows of the horses, but there weren't so many. She could also hear awkward steps of men whose days were spent in the saddle, now combing every inch of the ground below. Now and then she could hear someone mutter.

"This is my last time," one of the searchers confided to a companion. "I'm gittin' my money and gittin' out."

"Me, too. Besides, Boss says we'd better lay low, anyway."

Hours later, Angela was roused by the return of the outfit. "Not a thing!" The man called Pete must have been the spokesman.

"You couldn't find a cow in a pasture!" Rags was up, and he was furious. Angela could see his dark face in the glow of the fire Jasper had made in front of the cabin.

"You couldn't have done no better," a voice retorted. "She can't get far before mornin'. We'll catch her then."

"Yeah." Another hand chimed in, holding his hands out to the fire. "You saw what she had on her feet. She ain't going to be doin' much walkin' tonight."

Rags threw up his hands. "Oh, all right! Come eat. I fixed some grub."

The fare may have been plain and coarse, but to the tired, hungry girl in the tree, the aroma was almost unbearable. She had had nothing to eat since leaving the cabin that morning. Now it must be long after midnight.

"Wonder how come Slim ain't here?" Rags said.

"Aw, he probably got the gal to tell him where that gold was. Then he'd grab the gold and ride off some other direction!"

"An' leave the gal? Haw haw!"

"Shut up. I heard a horse."

Angela strained her ears. There was no sound.

"You heard one of ours."

"Guess yer right." Jasper paced back and forth in front of the fire, casting a grotesque shadow. "Rags, shouldn't we split up? Let the boys get the cattle movin'. We can't wait for daylight. You and me can stay here and catch the gal and wait for Slim."

Rags grunted in agreement. "Yeah. Better get out of here. I ain't too keen on this business about Slim and the gal. Pete, Shorty, you take the boys and get those cattle to Minerstown. We'll be there later and drive

208

to Tuttle's. Then it's every man fer himself. Spread out. When it's safe I'll get in touch."

Even from the distance above, Angela could hear suspicion in Pete's voice. "An' how about our pay?"

"You'll get it at Tuttle's."

"Okay, hands, hit the trail!"

Angela's weary eyelids drooped, but she was roused by Rags' voice. "I made up my mind. I'm goin' to take the gal."

Jasper sharply dumped the rest of his coffee on the fire. "You crazy? We can't take a gal on this drive!"

"I ain't takin' her on the drive. When Slim comes with the gold, I'm goin' to kill him and ride off with the gal. You can ride after the boys and settle with them at Tuttle's."

"An' leave you with all the gold."

How could Rags fail to hear the bite in his companion's words?

"We've been friends for a long time, ain't we, Rags?"

"Yeah. So what?"

"So I'm tellin' you there's somethin' queer about this deal. Better let the gal go. She can't crawl out of here alive, anyway. She made it once, but her feet must've been torn to ribbons. She don't know nothin' anyhow. Let's get out of here right now, before Slim gets back."

"An' let him have the gold and the girl?"

"Yeah." Jasper's face was hard in the fire-light. "There are other gals and gold. This deal stinks."

"Hands up!"

Angela nearly fainted. The voice was Will Clark's.

The two men at the fire froze, then simultaneously sprang toward the cabin. A volley of shots rang out, cutting off their escape. Turning, they fired into the bushes where the bullets had come from. Angela heard a moan. Without thought for her own safety, she called out, "Will!" and scrambled down the tree. The moment her feet hit the ground, she raced around the cabin, shooting wildly until the gun she carried was empty. Throwing it down, she snatched the other from her dress.

"Whoa, there!" Will's face gleamed in the firelight. "It's all over, little school-marm."

"Will, thank God!" Her arms encircled him as she looked up at him. Will wrapped his arms around her, holding her close.

"Angel!" Their first kiss was sweet, more so because of the terrible ordeal Angela had gone through.

Someone coughed and Angela broke free, her hands covering her face in embarrassment. Red Taggart was standing before her, grinning.

"Beggin' your pardon, ma'am, but — this ain't all of 'em, is it?"

Angela's newly found joy faded as she saw the two horribly crumpled figures in front of the fire.

"No —" She resolutely turned back to Red. "There are eight or nine more." Her words came in a rush, tumbling out over one another. "They're driving the last of the cattle to Minerstown, then to Tuttle's. They've got another big bunch of cattle being held at Minerstown. This is their last big drive."

Red's face darkened, and he slapped his sombrero back on his flaming hair. "Then I reckon we'll be chasin' after them." His eyes met Will's. "You take the Angel home."

"In a pig's eye!" Will confronted Red, his eyes flashing. "Think I'll let you go without me?" He hesitated, then added, "Especially seein' as how those cows are half mine."

"*What!*" Red looked as if Will had taken leave of his senses. "Yours! You loco?"

"Nope. Bought half interest in Owlhoot's ranch. The Double O's half mine now." He grinned as Red's mouth dropped open. "No, I didn't hold up a stage. Folks left me the money. Now, let's ride."

"Will, don't go!" Angela threw herself into his arms. "If you leave me now —" Her voice failed her. For a moment, she felt him weaken, then —

"Sorry, Angel. Obe and Jed will take you home. I've got a job to do." Firmly, he set her aside. For the first time, she was aware of the others — the sheriff, Owlhoot, the Siller boys.

"One of their bullets grazed Obe," Will said. "Fix his arm and go home with them. I'll come when I can." The steady blue eyes never wavered.

"You don't have to worry about meetin' Slim. He won't be botherin' anyone." The chill from his words seemed to sink into her bones, but, before she could speak, the men were gone. Only the Siller boys and the gruesome shapes by the fire remained.

Angela was torn between the desire to go after Will and the desire to obey his command. She turned to Obe and saw blood dripping from his left arm. He looked oddly calm and unconcerned.

"I'll wrap this for you, Obe." She turned toward Jed. "Give me your kerchief. It will have to do until we can get to something better. I left my petticoats halfway between here and Outlaw Junction." She ignored Jed's gasp and bound Obe's arm.

"You can ride Burnt Sugar," Jed said and helped her mount. When they rode down the valley, now lit by soft moonlight, Angela never looked back. For the first time since escaping from the cabin, she felt the pain searing through her feet. It took all her willpower just to hang on to her horse.

"I wish they'd let me go with them," Jed said.

Angela's misery was eclipsed by the wistfulness in his voice. "They knew I needed you more than they did, Jed," she said gently.

Jed perked up. "Yeah. We've got to get out of here and get Obe home."

How Angela ever managed to cling to Burnt Sugar, she never knew. The hours were a blur of pain and shadow, moonlight and weariness. Once she roused to hear Obe ask, "Reckon she's going to marry Will Clark, Jed?"

"I reckon she is. She was kissin' him when I got there."

"Then I won't even speak for her. No reason to."

Angela would never forget the loyal reply. "She met Will first, Obe. Otherwise she would have been proud to have you."

"What if he don't come back?" Angela's terrible fear subsided at Jed's quiet reply.

"He will. Wouldn't you — if you knew she was waitin'?"

Tears stung Angela's weary eyes.

"Angel — Miss Cartwright," Obe caught up with Burnt Sugar. "You all right?"

"I'm all right. Do you — Will said Slim wouldn't be bothering anyone anymore —"

"He won't. He's dead."

"Dead!" Angela sat straight up in the saddle. "Who killed him?"

"I reckon Red Taggart. Slim came to the school an—"

Jed shot a warning look at his brother. "An' Red had to kill him." He hurried on. "He found the gold."

"The gold!"

"Yeah. Part of the fightin' was in the school. Slim must have fallen over the stove, knocked down the stovepipe and the bag fell out."

Angela shuddered. "I don't ever want to see that gold — not after all that's happened."

"Sure, you feel like that now. You'll forget all this when Will Clark comes back." The boy's voice dropped to a whisper. "Wish I had some of that gold. I'd git me a harmonica like yers."

Angela laughed wildly, a sound harsh in the night. "Jed, I promise I'll get you and Obe both harmonicas, a lot better than

214

mine." Feeling lightheaded, she clutched the reins to keep her balance. "You deserve that and a lot more."

"If you want to give some more of it away, I heard Doc Bennett sayin' the other day he sure wished he had money to get some new-fangled doctorin' stuff."

Angela stirred. "That's what I can do! We can get maps and supplies for our school, too."

"Reckon you won't be teachin' us anymore if you git hitched to Will Clark."

"I don't know." Angela drooped down into the saddle. "Jed, I don't think I can ride anymore."

The boy was at her side immediately. "You hang onto me. We're almost home."

Was it minutes or hours before Angela saw the dark outline of the Siller cabin? Jed called, "Pa, Ma, git up. Obe's hurt, and the Angel's with us."

A flare of light illuminated the doorway and a grizzled man and stooped woman came out. "Get down, miss." Rough hands helped her. "We ain't got much, but yer welcome to what there is."

"Mr. Siller, could you possibly take me to the Double O?" She saw the disapproval in his dark eyes. "Mom Olson — she'll be worried."

The eyes softened. "Shore. We've got a wagon. Jed, git it hitched."

"Miss Angel, are you hungry?"

"Mrs. Siller, I'm starved!" Angela saw the pleased look in the woman's eyes.

"I've got some corn pone and sweet milk, if that'd be all right. It ain't much, but you can eat it while Jed hitches up."

"It sounds wonderful." Angela hobbled into the cabin. It was starkly furnished, but spotless. The corn pone and milk were a feast.

"Come back and see us," Mrs. Siller invited.

On impulse, Angela put her arms around the gaunt woman. "I will, Mrs. Siller. And thank you." It was the last conscious thought she had until Mr. Siller helped her out of the wagon at the Double O.

"She's all right, Mrs. Olson. Her feet are cut up pretty bad and she's tuckered out, but she's all right."

Mom Olson's soft cry only half-registered, but Angela roused enough to say weakly, "They're all right — all of them," before falling back into Mr. Siller's arms.

"Carry her upstairs for me, please, Mr. Siller." Mom was in command.

When Angela finally opened her heavy eyelids, the room was in shadow. She wrinkled her nose. What time was it? A glance at the clock brought her upright in bed. Nine o'clock? At night? Had she slept the entire day?

"Angel? You awake?" Mom Olson stuck her head in the door.

"I think so."

"Sit up and eat something."

Angela tried to swing her feet out of bed. They wouldn't move. Mom chuckled. "Don't try to move those feet. Doc Bennett came out today and looked at them. He bandaged them and said you weren't to stand until tomorrow."

"Mom?" The color drained from Angela's face. "Is Will — are the boys back?"

"Not yet." Mom quickly added, "Now, don't you go worryin' none. It's quite a piece to Tuttle's and back. I don't expect them until sometime tomorrow, maybe late. They'll have to drive all those cattle back after they catch them."

"What if —"

"We don't talk about any what-ifs. They'll be here when their job's done." She deftly fed Angela a spoon of hearty soup. "You want to tell me what happened?"

"I don't know where to start."

Mom laughed. "At the beginnin's a good place."

The story was interrupted only by Mom's occasional, "Well, now!" or "I wouldn't have thought it." When the recital was over she rose.

"You get back to sleep. I've got a hunch that when Will comes, he's goin' to be just a little anxious to see you."

While the Sillers were taking Angela home, the Double O hands were riding hard. "Best thing is to take 'em by surprise," Will told the sheriff and Owlhoot.

His body might be chasing cattle thieves up that steep and winding canyon, but his heart remained with a bright-haired girl who'd been through God-knew-what. He hadn't even had time to hear her story. He felt a pang as he remembered how she had pleaded with him to stay. For a split second he had been tempted, but he had to go with Red and Owlhoot and the others. Not even for The Arizona Angel could he turn his back on his partners when there was danger ahead.

"The way I figure, they got about two to three hours start." Owlhoot's voice snapped Will to attention. "They're drivin' cattle so we can make better time. We should git to Minerstown about the same time they do."

"Red!" Will called to his friend. "You

know any shortcuts to Minerstown?"

Red scratched his head. "Yeah!" His lips stretched in a grin. "There's that cutoff by Tony's Well. Probably ain't in good shape, but passable. It cuts off in about three miles."

"Good. That should put us there ahead of 'em. They won't be so likely to put up a fight."

"You're gettin' smarter all the time."

Will waited until the whole outfit caught up. "We're goin' by way of Tony's Well. We'll hole up in Minerstown before they get there and then wait."

It was broad daylight before the Double O hands reached Minerstown. It had taken longer than they figured. The old trail had been almost non-existent.

"They're already here," Red hissed. "See? They're just gettin' ready to drive the new bunch of cows in with the others."

"All right, men," Will said, "split up. Surround the corral, but don't shoot until I do. Maybe we won't even have to."

Will waited until he knew the outfit had found cover and surrounded the corral. *"Get your hands up, you side-winding cattle rustlers!"* He leaped into the open.

"The Double O!" Pete and Shorty dropped flat, and let a barrage of bullets fly.

Will felt a sharp pain in his shoulder. Raising his Colt, he snapped a quick shot toward the corral. It was followed by a dozen others.

"Hold it! They got us covered!" A voice from inside a rude shelter rang out. "I'm comin' out."

"Put your hands up," Red ordered. "Line up over against those bars." The sweating rustlers did as ordered. "Shall we string 'em up?"

The sheriff stepped forward. "Naw. We'll take 'em in and ship 'em off where they belong. Twenty years on a rock pile might take some of the meanness out of 'em."

Red scowled. "I still think we ought'a hang 'em."

"Swede, Vaq, tie 'em up," the sheriff ordered. "Owlhoot, looks like you and Will and Red are the only ones who got nicked. We'll take care of these hombres and git your cattle home. You go on."

"What about Tuttle?" The fire in Red's eyes still flickered.

"Can't prove a thing. I'll mosey over and have a little talk with him when we finish here."

With a gleam in his eye, Red said, "Can't prove nothin' on Tuttle. Why not hang these feller's hides on his corral as a warnin'? 'Course, if they wanted to talk —"

"We'll talk." A dark-haired man pushed forward, closely followed by the others. "No use of us croakin' 'cause of Tuttle."

One of the others grabbed the speaker's arm. "And just what do you think Rags and Jasper'll do if we squeal?"

"They're both dead." Red waved his gun again. "You fellers got somethin' to say?"

The leader whipped around to the sheriff. "If we talk, will you give us twenty-four hours to get away?"

"Well, now," the sheriff said, "if you're so all-fired anxious to talk and if you're willing to get out of Arizona, I reckon we could make a deal."

"Tuttle's the buyer. No questions. Cash for whatever we take him." The leader seemed eager to get it out and get away. Keeping one eye on Red Taggart's gun, he answered the sheriff's sharp questions. What he said provided damning evidence against Tuttle.

Will felt a little sick when it was all over. He hated bloodshed. All he wanted was to get back to the Double O. "Better tie up my shoulder, Owlhoot. The slug went clear through, and we've got a ways to ride. Your hand okay?"

"Fine." Owlhoot fashioned a crude ban-

221

dage and bound it tightly in place. "Good thing it's your left shoulder." He moved on to Red. "You're just grazed. Here, your hat will keep it from bleedin' any more. Let's go."

The sorry-looking trio headed back the way they'd come. "Wish there was a shortcut to the Double O," Owlhoot said with a worried look at Will. "That shoulder doesn't look too good."

"It's fine." Will bit his lips, denying the throbbing pain that pounded through his body with every heartbeat. But by the time they made it back to Hidden Canyon, he was feverish.

"We've got to git that wound washed out," Owlhoot ordered. "There's water here, and grub. We'll hole up a day or two."

"I'll just get rid of our friends here." Red grimaced and walked toward the stiff bodies of Rags and Jasper. "I hate diggin', but somebody's got to bury them. You take care of Will."

"Fine thing," Will growled. "Laid up from a hole in the shoulder!"

Owlhoot was gentle as he washed and rebandaged Will's arm, and Will managed to drop into an uneasy sleep. Later, when he awakened, he hobbled to the door and grinned. Owlhoot and Red were huddled in

222

blankets, snoring loudly.

"Tomorrow —" Will told the cold stars, "tomorrow I'm goin' home." His mind filled with a vision of Angela in her tattered skirt, her gun blazing. He smiled, but slowly a worrisome question began to take shape in his mind. He would have to wait through the night to get the answer.

"Red," Will said, as the men prepared to mount up for the long ride home, "did you notice just how Rags and Jasper died?"

"What are you gettin' at?"

Will swallowed hard. "The Angel came around the cabin, shootin' mighty straight. Way I figure, she saved some of our lives. But she ain't goin' to want to know she killed anyone."

Red's eyes were veiled. "She don't have to know."

Owlhoot broke the little silence. "Way *I* figure is that it was my bullets that killed them. 'Course, that's just how *I* figure."

"How come?" Red's eyes narrowed.

"The Angel also ain't going to want to know that you boys, especially Will here, killed anyone. Funny, what bad shots you turned out to be."

"What about Mom?"

Owlhoot's gaze riveted on the far horizon. "Mom was born and bred in this country.

We've been here a long time. It's different with the Angel." He swung onto his horse. "Let's go home."

Toward the end of their ride, they stopped at the Sillers. They made sure Obe was okay and that Angela had gone to the Double O. In spite of their weariness, they picked up speed as they finally reached the boundaries of the Double O. The big gate lay just ahead.

"Halloo, Mom!" Owlhoot's call brought a figure to the porch that waved and disappeared back inside. A moment later, a second figure joined her. She was slighter and dressed in white.

Owlhoot chuckled. "Mom must've found somethin' for her to wear. This should be good — she's about half Mom's size!"

"Sure wish I had an angel waitin' for me," Red said without rancor. He watched as the smaller figure ran across the porch and disappeared into the trees. "What's she runnin' away for?"

Will's heart dropped. Angela must have been expressing only gratitude when she embraced him in the canyon. Why else would she look at them now and run? His heart felt like an anvil as his dreams crashed. He had been a fool to think a girl like her could ever care for him. In pain and misery, he rode up to the porch, forcing himself to smile at Mom.

Owlhoot didn't hesitate. "Where did the Angel go?"

Mom's eyes twinkled. "She's been watchin' for you all day. I reckon the looks of you scared her to death. She ran off in the trees. Don't see how — her feet are still in bad shape."

Will was suddenly tired. "I think I'll go to my cabin."

"Need any help?" Red's eyes were knowing.

"No. I'll rustle over later for some food." Will dropped from Apple Pie. "I'd appreciate it if you'd take care of Apple Pie." He started toward his cabin.

So it had all been just a fancy, dreaming of how he'd come home to the Double O and Angela. Was she another Ellen Sue, running away from him? All he wanted was to be alone. But would he ever be alone now that he loved the Angel? Would her red-gold hair, her red lips always haunt his memory?

The last ray of sunlight was touching his cabin. He paused on the porch, dreading the emptiness. Then a figure stepped to the doorway, filling it with welcome. Red-gold hair swirled over a white gown.

"Angel?" He leaped to the doorstep and

peered down at her.

Red lips tempted, white arms invited, and a rippling laugh filled the silence between them. "You — you told me to get a white dress ready. It won't do for Parson Riley, but I thought —"

His painful shoulder forgotten, Will wrapped her in his arms, crushing her laughing lips beneath his own in a kiss that ended with hearts beating in time.

"You've never said — said you loved me," Will held his breath, waiting.

"I love you, Will." She nestled in his arms and whispered, "It's all been worth it — to find you."

"Angel!" His face was transfixed as a shaft of light from the departing sun lit up the spot where they stood, pronouncing a glorious benediction on Will and his own Arizona Angel.

We hope you have enjoyed this Large Print book. Other Thorndike Press or Chivers Press Large Print books are available at your library or directly from the publishers.

For more information about current and upcoming titles, please call or write, without obligation, to:

Thorndike Press
295 Kennedy Memorial Drive
Waterville, ME 04901 USA
Tel. (800) 223-1244
Tel. (800) 223-6121

OR

Chivers Press Limited
Windsor Bridge Road
Bath BA2 3AX
England
Tel. (0225) 335336

All our Large Print titles are designed for easy reading, and all our books are made to last.